DEFINITELY MAYBE

ARKADY (1925–1991) and **BORIS** (1933–2012) **STRUGATSKY** were the most acclaimed and beloved science fiction writers of the Soviet era. The brothers were born and raised in Leningrad, the sons of a critic and a teacher. When the city was besieged by the Germans during World War II, Arkady and their father, Natan, were evacuated to the countryside. Boris remained in Leningrad with their mother throughout the war. Arkady was drafted into the Soviet army and studied at the Military Institute of Foreign Languages, graduating in 1949 as an interpreter from English and Japanese. He served as an interpreter in the Far East before returning to Moscow in 1955. Boris studied astronomy at Leningrad State University, and worked as an astronomer and computer engineer. In the mid-1950s, the brothers began to write fiction, and soon published their first jointly written novel, *From Beyond*. They would go on to write twenty-five novels together, including *Roadside Picnic*, which was the basis for Andrei Tarkovsky's film *Stalker*; *Snail on the Slope*; *Hard to Be a God*; and *Monday Begins on Saturday*, as well as numerous short stories, essays, plays, and film scripts. Their books have been translated into multiple languages and published in twenty-seven countries. After Arkady's death in 1991, Boris continued writing, publishing two books under the name S. Vititsky. Boris died on November 19, 2012, at the age of seventy-nine. The asteroid 3054 Strugatskia, discovered in 1977, the year *Definitely Maybe* was first published, is named after the brothers.

ANTONINA W. BOUIS has translated many Russian writers, including Yevgeny Yevtushenko, Tatyana Tolstoya, Sergei Dovlatov, and Andrei Sakharov.

THE NEVERSINK LIBRARY

I was by no means the only reader of books on board the Neversink. Several other sailors were diligent readers, though their studies did not lie in the way of belles-lettres. Their favourite authors were such as you may find at the book-stalls around Fulton Market; they were slightly physiological in their nature. My book experiences on board of the frigate proved an example of a fact which every book-lover must have experienced before me, namely, that though public libraries have an imposing air, and doubtless contain invaluable volumes, yet, somehow, the books that prove most agreeable, grateful, and companionable, are those we pick up by chance here and there; those which seem put into our hands by Providence; those which pretend to little, but abound in much. —HERMAN MELVILLE, WHITE JACKET

DEFINITELY MAYBE
A MANUSCRIPT DISCOVERED UNDER STRANGE CIRCUMSTANCES

ARKADY AND BORIS STRUGATSKY

TRANSLATED BY ANTONINA W. BOUIS
AFTERWORD BY BORIS STRUGATSKY

MELVILLE HOUSE PUBLISHING
BROOKLYN · LONDON

DEFINITELY MAYBE

Originally published under the title *За миллиард лет
до конца света* [*One Billion Years to the End of the World*]
Copyright © 1976, 1977 by Arkady and Boris Strugatsky
Translation copyright © 1978 by Macmillan Publishers Ltd.
Afterword copyright © 2013 by the Estates of Boris and Arkady Strugatsky
Translation of the afterword copyright © 2013 by Antonina W. Bouis

First Melville House printing: February 2014

Melville House Publishing   8 Blackstock Mews
145 Plymouth Street   and   Islington
Brooklyn, NY 11201   London N4 2BT

mhpbooks.com   facebook.com/mhpbooks   @melvillehouse

Library of Congress
Cataloging-in-Publication Data

Strugatskii, Arkadii, 1925–1991.
  [*Za milliard let do kontsa sveta*. English]
  Definitely maybe : a manuscript discovered under strange
circumstances / Arkady Strugatsky and Boris Strugatsky ;
translated by Antonia W. Bouis.
     pages   cm
  ISBN 978-1-61219-281-9 (pbk.)
  ISBN 978-1-61219-282-6 (ebook)
  I. Strugatskii, Boris, 1933–2012, author. II. Bouis, Antonina
W., translator. III. Title.

PG3476.S78835Z3213 2014
891.73'44—dc23

                                        2013038567

Design by Christopher King

Printed in the United States of America
1 3 5 7 9 10 8 6 4 2

DEFINITELY MAYBE
A MANUSCRIPT DISCOVERED UNDER
STRANGE CIRCUMSTANCES

CHAPTER 1

Excerpt 1.... the white July heat, the hottest it had been in two hundred years, engulfed the city. The air shimmered over red-hot rooftops. All the windows in the city were flung open, and in the thin shade of wilting trees, old women sweated and melted on benches near courtyard gates.

The sun charged past the meridian and sank its claws into the long-suffering book bindings and the glass and polished wood of the bookcases; hot, angry patches of reflected light quivered on the wallpaper. It was almost time for the afternoon siege, for the furious sun to hang dead still in the sky above the twelve-story house across the street and fire endless rounds of heat into the apartment.

Malianov closed the window—both frames—and drew the heavy yellow drapes. Then, hitching up his underpants, he padded over to the kitchen in his bare feet and opened the door to the balcony. It was just after two.

On the kitchen table, among the bread crumbs, was a still life consisting of a frying pan with the dried-up remains of an omelet, an unfinished glass of tea, and a gnawed end of bread smeared with oozing butter.

"No one's washed up and nothing is washed," Malianov said to himself.

The sink was overflowing with unwashed dishes. They hadn't been done in a long time.

The floorboard squeaked, and Kaliam appeared out of no-where, mad with the heat; he glanced up at Malianov with his green eyes and soundlessly opened and closed his mouth. Then, tail twitching, he proceeded to his dish under the oven. There was nothing on his dish except a few bare fish bones.

"You're hungry," Malianov said unhappily.

Kaliam immediately replied in a way that meant, well, yes, it wouldn't hurt to have a little something.

"You were fed this morning," said Malianov, crouching in front of the refrigerator. "Or no, that's not right. It was yester-day morning I fed you."

He took out Kaliam's pot and looked into it—there were a couple of scraps and a fish fin stuck to the side. There wasn't even that much in the refrigerator itself. There was an empty box that used to have some Yantar cheese in it, a horrible-looking bottle with the dregs of kefir, and a wine bottle filled with iced tea. In the vegetable bin, amid the onion skins, a wrinkled piece of cabbage the size of a fist lay rotting and a sprouting potato languished in oblivion. Malianov looked into the freezer—a tiny piece of bacon on a plate had settled in for the winter among the mountains of frost. And that was it.

Kaliam was purring and rubbing his whiskers on Mali-anov's bare knee. Malianov shut the refrigerator and stood up.

"It's all right," he told Kaliam. "Everything's closed for lunch now, anyway."

Of course, he could go over to Moscow Boulevard, where the break was from one to two. But there were always lines there, and it was too far to go in this heat. And then, what a crummy integral that turned out to be! Well, all right, let that be the constant ... it doesn't depend on omega. It's clear that it doesn't. It follows from the most general considera-tions that it doesn't. Malianov imagined the sphere and pic-tured the integration traveling over the entire surface. Out of nowhere Zhukovsky's formula popped into his mind. Just like that. Malianov chased it away, but it came back. Let's try the conformal representation, he thought.

The phone rang again, and Malianov found himself back in the living room, much to his surprise. He swore, flopped down on the sofa, and reached over for the phone.

"Yes."

"Vitya?" asked an energetic female voice.

"What number do you want?"

"Is this Intourist?"

"No, a private apartment."

Malianov hung up and lay still for a while, feeling the nap of the blanket against his naked side and beginning to drip with sweat. The yellow shade glowed, filling the room with an unpleasant yellow light. The air was like gelatin. He should move into Bobchik's room, that's what. This room was a steambath. He looked at his desk, heaped with papers and books. There were six volumes just of Vladimir Ivanovich Smirnov. And all those papers scattered on the floor. He shuddered at the thought of moving. Wait a minute, I had a breakthrough before. Damn you and your stupid Intourist, you stupid blockhead. Let's see, I was in the kitchen and then I ended up in here. Oh yes! Conformal representation! A stupid idea. But I guess it should be looked into.

He got up from the bed with a low groan, and the phone rang again.

"Idiot," he said to the phone and picked it up. "Hello?"

"Is this the depot? Who's on the phone? Is this the depot?"

Malianov hung up and dialed the repair service.

"Hello? My number is nine-three-nine-eight-zero-seven. Listen, I already called you last night. I can't work, I keep getting wrong numbers."

"What's your number?" a vicious female voice interrupted.

"Nine-three-nine-eight-zero-seven. I keep getting calls for Intourist and the depot and—"

"Hang up. We'll check it."

"Please do," Malianov said to the dial tone.

Then he slapped over to the table, sat down, and picked up his pen. So-o-o, where did I see that integral? Such a neat little guy symmetrical on all sides ... where did I see it? And not even a constant, just a plain old zero! Well, all right then. Let's leave it in the rearguard. I don't like leaving anything in the rear, it's as unpleasant as a rotting tooth.

He began rechecking the previous night's calculations and he suddenly felt good. It was pretty clever, by God! That Malianov! What a mind! Finally, you're getting there. And, brother, it looks good. This was no routine "figure of the pivots in a large transit instrument"; this was something that no one had ever done before! Knock on wood. This integral. Damn the integral, full speed ahead!

There was a ring. The doorbell. Kaliam jumped down from the bed and raced to the foyer with his tail in the air. Malianov neatly set down his pen.

"They're out in full force," he said.

Kaliam traced impatient circles in the foyer, getting underfoot.

"Ka-al-liam!" Malianov said in a suppressed but threatening tone. "Get out of here, Kaliam!"

He opened the door. On the other side stood a shabby man, unshaven and sweaty, wearing a jacket of indeterminate color that was too small for him. Leaning back to balance the huge cardboard box he was holding, muttering something incomprehensible, he came straight at Malianov.

"You, er ..." Malianov mumbled, stepping aside.

The shabby fellow had already penetrated the foyer. He looked to the right, into the room, and turned determinedly to the left, into the kitchen, leaving dusty white footprints on the linoleum.

"Er, just a . . ." muttered Malianov, hot on his heels.

The man put the box down on a stool and pulled out a batch of receipts from his pocket.

"Are you from the Tenants' Committee, or what?" For some reason, Malianov thought that perhaps the plumber had finally shown up to fix the bathroom sink.

"From the deli," the man said hoarsely and handed him two receipts pinned together. "Sign here."

"What is this?" Malianov asked, and saw that they were order blanks. Cognac—two bottles; vodka . . . "Wait a minute, I don't think we ordered anything," he said.

He saw the tab. He panicked. He didn't have money like that in the apartment. And anyway, what was going on? His panic-stricken brain flashed vivid pictures of all kinds of complications, like explaining this away, refusing it, arguing, demanding, phoning the store, or maybe even going there in person. But then he saw the purple PAID stamp in the corner of the receipt and the name of the purchaser—I. E. Malianova. Irina! What the hell was going on?

"Just sign here," the shabby man insisted, pointing with his black nail. "Where the X is."

Malianov took the man's pencil stub and signed.

"Thanks," he said, returning the pencil. "Thanks a lot," he repeated, squeezing through the narrow foyer with the delivery man. I should give him something, but I don't have any change. "Thank you very much. So long!" he called to the back of the tight jacket, viciously pushing back Kaliam with his leg. The cat was trying to get outside to lick the cement floor of the landing.

Then Malianov closed the door and stood in the dusky light. His head was muddled.

"Strange," he said aloud, and went back to the kitchen.

Kaliam was rubbing his head against the box. Malianov lifted the cover and saw tops of bottles, packages, bags, and cans. The copy of the receipt was on the table. So. The carbon was smeared, as usual, but he could make out the handwriting. Hero Street ... hmm ... everything seemed to be in order. Purchaser: I. E. Malianova. That was a nice hello! He looked at the total again. Mind-boggling! He turned the receipt over. Nothing interesting on the other side. A squashed mosquito. What was the matter with Irina? Had she gone completely bananas? We're in debt for five hundred rubles. Wait, maybe she said something about this before she left? He tried to remember that day, the open suitcases, the mounds of clothes strewn all over the house, Irina half-dressed and wielding her iron. Don't forget to feed Kaliam, bring him some grass, the spiky kind; don't forget the rent; if my boss calls, give him my address. That seemed to be it. She had said something else, but Bobchik had run in with his machine gun. Oh yes! Take the sheets to the laundry. I don't understand a damn thing!

Malianov gingerly pulled a bottle out of the box. Cognac. At least fifteen rubles! Is it my birthday or something? When did Irina leave? Thursday, Wednesday, Tuesday. He bent back his fingers. It was ten days today that she left. That means she had placed the order ahead of time. Borrowed the money from somebody again and ordered it. A surprise. Five hundred in debt, you see, and she wants to give me a surprise! At least one thing was settled: he wouldn't have to go to the store. The rest was a fog as far as he was concerned. Birthday? No. Wedding anniversary? Didn't think so. No, definitely not. Bobchik's birthday? No, that's in the winter.

He counted the bottles. Ten of them. Who did she think would drink it all? I couldn't handle that much in a year!

Vecherovsky hardly drinks either, and she can't stand Val
Weingarten.

Kaliam began howling terribly. He sensed something in
the box.

Excerpt 2. . . . some salmon in its own juices and a piece of ham
with the stale crust of bread. Then he took on the dirty dishes.
It was perfectly clear that a dirty kitchen was particularly of-
fensive with such luxury in the refrigerator. The phone rang
twice during this time, but Malianov merely set his jaw more
firmly. I won't answer, and that's it. The hell with all of them
with their Intourist and depots. The frying pan will also have
to be cleaned, no getting around it. The pan will be needed
for goals higher than some crummy omelet. Now, what's the
crux here? If the integral is really zero, then all that remains
on the right side are the first and second derivatives. I don't
quite understand the physics of it, but it doesn't matter, it sure
makes terrific bubbles. Yes, that's what I'll call them: bubbles. No, "cavities" is probably better. The Malianov cavities.
"M cavities." Hmmm.

He put the dishes away and looked into Kaliam's pan. It
was still too hot. Poor Kaliam. He'll have to wait. Poor little
Kaliam will have to wait and suffer until it cools off.

He was wiping his hand when he was struck by an idea,
just like yesterday. And just like yesterday, he didn't believe it
at first.

"Wait a minute, wait just one minute," he muttered feverishly, while his legs carried him down the hallway with the
cool linoleum that stuck to his heels, through the thick yellow heat, to his desk and pen. Hell, where was it? Out of ink.
There was a pencil around here somewhere. And meanwhile
the secondary consideration, no, the primary, fundamental
consideration was Hartwig's function . . . and it was as though

the entire right part had disappeared. The cavities became axially symmetric—and the old integral wasn't zero! That is, it was so much not zero, the little integral, that the value was significantly positive. But what a picture it makes! Why didn't I figure this out long ago? It's all right, Malianov, relax, brother, you're not the only one. Old Academician whatsizname didn't figure it out either. In the yellow, slightly curved space, the axially symmetric cavities turned slowly like gigantic bubbles. Matter flowed around them, trying to seep through, but it couldn't. The matter compressed itself on the boundaries to such incredible densities that the bubbles began to glow. God knows what happens next—but we'll figure it out. First, we'll deal with the fiber structure. Then with Ragozinsky's arcs. And then with planetary nebulae. And what did you think, my friends? That these were expanding, thrown-off shells? Some shells! Just the opposite!

The damn phone rang again. Malianov roared in anger but went on writing. He should turn it off completely. There was a switch for that ... He threw himself down on the sofa and picked up the receiver.

"Yes!"

"Dmitri?"

"Yes, who's this?"

"You don't recognize me, you cur?" It was Weingarten.

"Oh, it's you, Val. What do you want?"

Weingarten hesitated.

"Why don't you answer your phone?"

"I'm working," Malianov said angrily. He was being very unfriendly. He wanted to get back to his table and see the rest of the picture with the bubbles.

"Working," Weingarten said. "Building your immortal edifice, I guess."

"What, did you want to drop by?"

"Drop by? No, not really."

Malianov lost his temper completely.

"Then what do you want?"

"Listen, pal ... What are you working on now?"

"I'm working. I told you."

"No ... I mean, what are you working *on*?"

Malianov was flabbergasted. He had known Val Weingarten for twenty-five years, and Weingarten had never expressed an iota of interest in Malianov's work. Weingarten had never been interested in anything but Weingarten himself with the exception of two mysterious objects: the 1934 twopenny and the "consul's half-ruble," which was not a half-ruble at all but some special postage stamp. The bum has nothing to do, Malianov decided. Just killing time. Or maybe he needs a roof over his head, and he's just building up to the question?

"What am I working on?" he asked with gleeful malice. "I can tell you in great detail if you like. You'll be fascinated by it all, I'm sure, being a biologist and all. Yesterday morning, I finally broke through. It turns out that in the most general assumptions regarding the potential function, my equations of motion have one more integral besides the integral of energy and the integrals of momenta. It's sort of a generalization of a limited three-field problem. If the equations of motion are given in vector form and then the Hartwig transformation is applied, then the integration is performed for the entire volume, and the whole problem is reduced to integro-differential equations of the Kolmogorov-Feller type."

To his vast amazement, Weingarten was not interrupting him. For a second, Malianov thought that they had been disconnected.

"Are you listening to me?"

"Yes, very attentively."

"Perhaps you even understand what I'm saying?"

"I'm getting some of it," Weingarten said heartily. Malianov suddenly realized how strange his voice was. He was frightened by it.

"Val, is something wrong?"

"What do you mean?" Weingarten asked, stalling.

"What do I mean? With you, of course! You sound a little funny. Can't you talk right now?"

"No, no, pal. That's nonsense. I'm all right. It's just the heat. Do you know the one about the two roosters?"

"No. Well?"

Weingarten told him the joke about two roosters—it was extremely dumb but rather funny. But not a Weingarten joke at all. Malianov, naturally, listened to it and laughed at the appropriate place, but the joke only intensified the vague feeling that all was not right with Weingarten. Maybe he'd had another round with Sveta, he thought uncertainly. Maybe they ruined his epithelium again. And then Weingarten asked:

"Listen, Dmitri. Does the name Snegovoi mean anything to you?"

"Snegovoi? Arnold Pavlovich Snegovoi? I have a neighbor by that name, lives across the hall. Why?"

Weingarten said nothing. He even stopped breathing through his mouth. There was only the sound of jingling and jangling—he must have been playing with his coins. "And what does he do, your Snegovoi?"

"A physicist, I think. Works in some bunker. Top secret. Where do you know him from?"

"I don't," Weingarten said with an inexplicable sadness. The doorbell rang.

"They're all champing at the bit!" Malianov said. "Hold on, Val. There's someone breaking down my door."

Weingarten said something, or even shouted, but Malianov had tossed the phone on the sofa and was running out into the foyer. Kaliam was underfoot already, and Malianov almost tripped over him.

He stepped back as soon as he opened the door. On his doorstep stood a young woman in a short white jumper, very tanned, with short sun-bleached hair. Beautiful. A stranger. (Malianov was acutely aware of wearing only his undershorts and having a sweaty belly.) There was a suitcase at her feet and a jacket over her arm.

"Dmitri Malianov?" she asked embarrassedly.

"Y-yes," Malianov answered. A relative? Third cousin Zina from Omsk?

"Please forgive me, Dmitri. I'm sure this isn't a good time for you. Here."

She handed him an envelope. Malianov silently took the envelope and removed a piece of paper from it. Horrible, wrathful feelings toward all the relatives in the world and specifically toward this Zina or Zoya raged in his chest.

But it turned out that this was no third cousin. In large hurried letters, the lines going this way and that, Irina had written: "Dimochka! This is Lida Ponomareva, my best friend from school. I told you about her. Be nice to her, don't growl. Won't stay long. Everything's fine. She'll tell you all about it. Kisses, I."

Malianov howled a long silent howl, closed his eyes, and opened them again. However, his lips were making an automatic, friendly smile.

"How nice," he said in a friendly, casual tone. "Come on in, Lida, please. Forgive my appearance. The heat, you know."

There must have been something wrong with his welcome, because Lida's pretty face took on a lost look, and for some reason she looked back out at the sunlit landing, as though suddenly questioning whether she had come to the right place.

"Here, let me take your suitcase," Malianov said quickly.

"Come in, come in, don't be shy. You can hang your jacket here. This is our main room, I work in there, and this is Bob-chik's. It will be yours. You probably want to take a shower?"

He heard a nasal quacking coming from the sofa.

"Sorry," he said. "Make yourself at home, I'll be right with you."

He grabbed the phone and heard Weingarten repeating in a strange monotone:

"Dmitri, Dmitri, oh, Dmitri, come to the phone, Dmitri."

"Hello! Val, listen—"

"Dmitri!" Weingarten shouted. "Is that you?"

Malianov was frightened.

"What are you shouting about? I've just had a visitor, for-give me. I'll call you later."

"Who? Who's the visitor?" Weingarten demanded in an inhuman voice.

Malianov felt a shiver. Val's gone mad. What a day.

"Val," he said very calmly. "What's the matter? A woman just arrived. A friend of Irina's."

"Son of a bitch!" said Weingarten and hung up.

CHAPTER 2

Excerpt 3.... and she changed from her minijumper into a miniskirt and a miniblouse. It must be said that she was a very attractive girl—and Malianov came to the conclusion she had no use for bras at all. She didn't need a bra; she was in perfect shape without one. He forgot all about the Malianov cavities.

But everything was very proper, the way it is in the best of homes. They sat and chatted and had tea, and sweated. He was Dimochka by then, and she was Lidochka for him. After the third glass Dimochka told her the joke about the two roosters—it just seemed appropriate—and Lidochka laughed merrily and waved her naked arm at Dimochka. He remembered (the roosters reminded him) that he was supposed to call Weingarten, but he didn't, instead he said to Lidochka:

"What a marvelous tan you have!"

"And you're as white as a slug," said Lidochka.

"Work, work, work."

"In the Pioneer camp where I work ..."

And Lidochka told him in minute detail, but with great charm, how it was in their Pioneer camp with regard to getting a tan. In return, Malianov told her how the fellows tan themselves on the Great Antenna. What was the Great Antenna? Hers was just to ask, and he told her about the Great Antenna. She stretched out her long brown legs, crossed them at the ankle, and put them on Bobchik's chair. Her legs were mirror-smooth. Malianov had the impression that they even reflected something. To get his mind off them, he got up and took the boiling teakettle off the stove. He managed to burn his fingers with the steam and was reminded of some monk who stuck an extremity into either fire or steam to escape the evil brewing as a result of his direct contact with a beautiful woman. A decisive fellow.

"How about another glass?" he asked.

Lidochka did not reply, and he turned around. She was looking at him with her wide-open, light eyes. There was a strange expression on her shiny tan face—not quite confusion and not quite fear—and her mouth was agape.

"Shall I pour some?" Malianov asked uncertainly, giving the kettle a wave.

Lidochka sat up, blinked rapidly, and brushed her forehead with her fingers.

"What?"

"I said: Would you like some more tea?"

"No, no, thanks." She laughed as if nothing had happened. "I have to watch my figure."

"Oh yes," Malianov said with extreme gallantry. "A figure like that has to be watched. Insured even."

She smiled briefly and, turning her head, looked out into the courtyard over her shoulder. She had a long, smooth neck, maybe just a bit too thin. Malianov had another impression. Namely, that the neck was created to be kissed. Just like her shoulders. And not even mentioning the rest. Circe, he thought. And immediately added: But I love my Irina and I will never be untrue to her in my whole life.

"That's strange," Circe said. "I have the feeling that I've seen all this before: this kitchen, this yard—only there was a big tree in the yard. Has that ever happened to you?"

"Of course." Malianov spoke readily. "I think it happens to everyone. I read somewhere that it's called *déjà vu*."

"Probably," she said doubtfully.

Malianov, trying not to make too much noise, sipped his tea carefully. There seemed to be a break in the banter. Something was worrying her.

"Perhaps you and I have already met somewhere?" she asked suddenly.

"Where? I would have remembered."

"Maybe accidentally. In the street or at a dance."

"A dance?" Malianov countered. "I've forgotten how to do it."

And they both stopped talking. So profound was the silence that Malianov's toes curled up in discomfort. It was that horrible situation when you don't know where to look and your brain is full of sentences that roll around like rocks in a barrel and are of absolutely no use in changing the subject or starting a new conversation. Like: "Our Kaliam goes right in the toilet bowl." Or "There just aren't any tomatoes in the stores this year." Or "How about another cup of tea?" Or, say, "Well, and how do you like our fair city?"

Malianov inquired in an unbearably false voice:

"Well, and what plans do you have for our fair city, Lidochka?"

She did not reply. She regarded him in silence, her eyes round in extreme surprise. Then she looked away, wrinkled her brow. Bit her lip. Malianov always considered himself a poor psychologist and usually had no inkling of anyone else's feelings. But it was perfectly clear to him that the question was beyond the beautiful Lida's ken.

"Plans?" she finally muttered. "Well, of course. Naturally!" She seemed to remember. "Well, the Hermitage, of course ... the Impressionists ... Nevsky Prospect ... and, you know, I've never seen the White Nights."

"A modest tourist itinerary," Malianov said quickly, helping her out. He couldn't watch a person trying to lie. "Let me pour you some tea."

And she laughed again, as cool as anything.

"Dimochka," she said, pouting her lips prettily. "Why are you pestering me with your tea? If you must know, I never drink the stuff. And especially in this heat!"

"Coffee?" Malianov offered readily.

She was categorically opposed to coffee. In the heat, and especially at bedtime, you shouldn't drink coffee. Malianov told her how the only thing that helped him in Cuba was drinking coffee—and the heat there was tropical. He explained about coffee's effect on the autonomic nervous system. And then he also told her, while he was at it, that in Cuba panties have to show under miniskirts, and if panties aren't visible, then it's not a miniskirt, and a woman whose panties are not visible, she is considered a nun and an old maid. For all that, the morality is, strangely, very strict. Uh-nuh! Revolution.

"What cocktails do they drink there?" she asked.

"Highballs," Malianov replied proudly. "Rum, sweet soda, and ice."

"Ice," she said dreamily . . .

Excerpt 4. . . . then he poured her another glass of wine. The decision to toast the use of the informal Russian personal pronoun for "you" came up. Without the kissing. Why should there be kissing between two intelligent people? The important thing was spiritual rapport. They drank to using the informal "you" and spoke of spiritual closeness, new methods of birth deliveries, and about the differences among courage, bravery, and valor. The Riesling was finished, and Malianov put the empty bottle out on the balcony and went over to the bar for some cabernet. They decided to drink the cabernet out of Irina's favorite smoked crystal glasses, which they chilled first. The conversation on femininity, which came up after the one on manliness and bravery, went very well with the icy red wine. They wondered what asses had decreed that red wine should never be chilled. They discussed the question. Isn't it true that iced red wine is particularly good? Yes, absolutely. By the way, women who drink icy red wine become particularly beautiful. They resemble witches somewhere. Where precisely? Somewhere. A marvelous word—*somewhere*. "You are a pig somewhere." I love that expression. By the way, speaking of witches—what do you think marriage is? A real marriage. An intelligent marriage. Marriage is a contract. Malianov refilled the glasses and developed the thought. In the aspect that a man and wife are first of all friends, for whom friendship is the most important thing. Honesty and friendship. Marriage is a friendship. A contract on friendship, understand? He had his hand on Lidochka's bare knee and was shaking it for emphasis. Take Irina and me. You know Irina—

The doorbell rang.

"Who could that be?" Malianov asked, looking at his watch. "Seems to me we're all home."

It was a little before ten. Repeating, "Seems to me we're all here," he went to open the door and naturally stepped on Kaliam in the foyer. Kaliam meowed.

"Ah, damn you, you devil!" Malianov said to him, and opened the door.

It turned out to be his neighbor, the highly mysterious Arnold Pavlovich Snegovoi.

"Is it too late?" he roared from under the ceiling. A huge man, built like a mountain. A gray-haired demon.

"Arnold!" Malianov said with glee. "What's the meaning of 'late' between friends? C'mon in!"

Snegovoi hesitated, sensing the cause of the glee, but Malianov grabbed his sleeve and dragged him into the foyer.

"You're just in time," he said, pulling Snegovoi on a tow-
line. "You'll meet a marvelous woman!" he promised as he
maneuvered Snegovoi around the corner into the kitchen. "Lidochka, this is Arnold!" he announced. "I'll just get another
glass, and another bottle."

Things were beginning to swim before his eyes. And not
just a little, if the truth be told. He shouldn't have anything
else to drink. He knew himself. But he really wanted things
to go well, for everyone to like everyone else. I hope they hit
it off, he thought generously, swaying in front of the opened
bar and peering into the yellow dusk. It's all right for him, he's
a bachelor. I have Irina. He shook his finger into space and
dived into the bar.

Thank God, he didn't break anything. When he came back
with a bottle of Bull's Blood and a clean glass, the situation in
the kitchen did not please him. They were both smoking in
silence without looking at each other. And for some reason
Malianov thought their faces were vicious: Lidochka's face was
viciously beautiful and Snegovoi's face, scarred by old burns,
was viciously stern.

"Who hushed the voice of joy?" Malianov asked. "Everything is nonsense! There is only one luxury in the world. The
luxury of human contact! I don't remember who said that." He
unscrewed the cork. "Let's enjoy the contact—the luxury..."

The wine flowed abundantly and all over the table. Snegovoi jumped up to protect his white pants. He was abnormally
large, he really was. People shouldn't be that big in our com-
pact times. Developing his thought, Malianov wiped the table.
Snegovoi sat back down on the stool. The stool crunched.

Up to that moment the luxury of human contact was being
expressed in garbled exclamations. Damn that shyness of the
intelligentsia! Two absolutely beautiful people cannot simply immediately open up to each other, take each other into

their hearts and minds, become friends from the very first second. Malianov stood up and, holding his glass at ear level, expounded the theme out loud. It didn't help. They drank. That didn't help either. Lidochka looked out the window in boredom. Snegovoi rolled his glass back and forth on the table between his huge brown hands. Malianov noticed for the first time that Arnold's arms were burned—all the way to the elbow, and even higher. This inspired him to ask:

"Well, Arnold, when will you disappear next?"

Snegovoi shuddered noticeably and looked up at him, then pulled his neck in and hunched his shoulders. Malianov got the impression that he was getting ready to get up, and he suddenly realized that his question, to put it mildly, may have appeared to have another meaning.

"Arnold!" he yelled, flinging his arms up toward the ceiling. "God, that's not at all what I meant! Lidochka, you must realize that this man is totally mysterious. He disappears from time to time. He drops by with the key to his place and melts into thin air. He'll be gone a month or two. And then the doorbell rings, and he's back." He felt that he was babbling, that it was enough, that it was time to change the subject. "Arnold, you know perfectly well that I really like you, and I'm always happy to see you. So there can't be any talk of your leaving before two in the morning."

"Of course, Dmitri," Snegovoi replied and slapped Malianov on the back. "Of course, my dear friend, of course."

"And this is Lidochka," Malianov announced, pointing in her direction. "My wife's best friend from school. From Odessa."

Snegovoi forced himself to turn toward Lidochka and asked: "Will you be in Leningrad long?"

She answered rather politely, and he asked another question, something about the White Nights.

In short, they began their luxurious contact, and Malianov could rest easy. No, no, I can't drink. What shame! I'm completely knocked out. Without hearing or understanding a single word, he watched Snegovoi's horrible face, eaten away by the fires of hell, and suffered pangs of conscience. When the suffering became unbearable, he got up quietly; clutching the walls, he made his way to the bathroom and locked himself in. He sat on the edge of the tub in gloomy despair for a while, then turned on the cold water full force and stuck his head under it.

When he got back, refreshed and with a wet collar, Snegovoi was in the middle of a tense rendition of the joke about the two roosters. Lidochka was laughing loudly, throwing her head back and exposing her made-for-kissing neck. Malianov took this as a good sign, even though he was not well disposed toward people who raised politeness to an art. However, the luxury of contact, like any other luxury, demanded certain expenditures. He waited while Lidochka laughed, picked up the falling banner and launched into a series of astronomical jokes that neither of the others could possibly have heard. When he ran out of jokes, Lidochka brightened the occasion with beach jokes. To tell the truth, the jokes were rather middling, and she didn't know how to tell them, either, but she did know how to laugh, and her teeth were sparkling sugar-white. Then the conversation somehow moved on to foretelling the future. Lidochka informed them that a gypsy woman told her that she would have three husbands and no children. What would we do without gypsies? muttered Malianov, and he bragged that a gypsy had told him that he would make a major discovery in the interrelation of stars with diffusion matter in the galaxy. They had some more iced Bull's Blood and then Snegovoi suddenly unburdened himself of a strange story.

It seems that he had been told that he would die at the age of eighty-three in Greenland. ("In the Socialist Republic of Greenland," Malianov joked, but Snegovoi replied calmly, "No, just in Greenland.") He believed in it fatally, and his conviction irritated everyone around him. Once, during the war, though not at the front, one of his friends, soused, or as they used to say in those days, blotto, was so maddened by it all that he pulled out his gun, stuck the barrel into Snegovoi's temple, and said, "Now we'll see," and cocked the gun.

"And?" Lidochka asked.

"Killed him dead," Malianov joked.

"It misfired," Snegovoi explained.

"You have some strange friends," Lidochka said doubtfully.

She hit it right on the barrelhead. Arnold Snegovoi rarely talked about himself, but when he did, it was memorable. And if one could judge by his stories, he had very strange friends indeed.

Then Malianov and Lidochka argued hotly for some time over how Arnold might end up in Greenland. Malianov leaned toward the airplane crash theory. Lidochka subscribed to the simple tourist vacation. As for Arnold himself, he sat, his purple lips pulled into a smile, smoking cigarette after cigarette.

Then Malianov thought about it and tried to pour some more wine into their glasses, but discovered that the bottle was already empty. He was about to rush over for another one, but Arnold stopped him. It was time for him to go, he had just stopped by for a minute. Lidochka, on the other hand, was ready to go on. She wasn't even tipsy, the only sign of the wine was her flushed cheeks.

"No, no, friends," said Snegovoi. "I have to go." He stood up heavily and filled the kitchen with his bulk. "I'm off. Why don't you see me out, Dmitri. Good night, Lidochka, it was nice meeting you."

They walked through the foyer. Malianov was still trying to talk him into staying for another bottle, but Snegovoi kept shaking his gray head resolutely and muttering negatively. In the doorway he said loudly:

"Oh yes! Dmitri! I had promised you that book. Come on over, I'll give it to you."

"What book?" Malianov was about to ask, but Snegovoi put his fat finger to his lips and pulled Malianov across the landing. The fat finger on the lips stunned Malianov, and he followed Snegovoi like a moth after a flame. Silently, still holding Malianov by the arm, Snegovoi found his key in his pocket and unlocked the door. The lights were on in the apartment—in the foyer, in both rooms, in the kitchen, and even in the bathroom. It smelled of stale tobacco and strong cologne, and Malianov suddenly realized that in the five years they had known each other, he had never been in here. The room that Snegovoi led him into was clean and neat; all the lamps were on—the three-bulb chandelier, the floor lamp in the corner by the couch, and the small table lamp. On the back of a chair hung a tunic with silver buttons and epaulets, with a whole slew of medals, bars, and decorations. It turned out that Arnold Snegovoi was a colonel. How about that?

"What book?" Malianov finally asked.

"Any book," Snegovoi said impatiently. "Here, take this one, and hold on to it or you'll forget it. Let's sit down for a minute."

Completely confused, Malianov took a thick tome from the table. Holding it tight under his arm, he sank onto the couch under the lamp. Arnold sat down next to him and lit a cigarette. He did not look at Malianov.

"So, it's like this . . . well . . ." he began. "First of all, who is that woman?"

"Lidochka? I told you. My wife's friend. Why?"

"Do you know her well?"

"No. I just met her today. She arrived with a letter." Malianov stopped short and asked in fright, "Why, do you think she's—"

"I'll ask the questions. We don't have the time. What are you working on now, Dmitri?"

Malianov remembered Val Weingarten and broke out in a cold sweat. He said with a wry grin:

"Everybody seems to be interested in my work today."

"Who else?" Snegovoi demanded, his little blue eyes boring into him. "Her?"

Malianov shook his head.

"No. Weingarten. A friend of mine."

"Weingarten. Weingarten." Snegovoi repeated.

"No, no!" Malianov said. "I know him well, we were in grammar school together, and we're still friends."

"Does the name Gubar mean anything to you?"

"Gubar? No. What's wrong, Arnold?"

Snegovoi put out his cigarette and lit another one.

"Who else made inquiries about your work?"

"No one else."

"So what are you working on?"

Malianov got angry. He always got angry when he was frightened.

"Listen, Arnold. I don't understand."

"Neither do I! And I want to know, very much. Tell me! Wait a minute. Is your work classified?"

"What do you mean classified?" Malianov said in irritation. "It's plain ordinary astrophysics and stellar dynamics. The interrelation of stars and interstellar matter. Nothing secret here, it's just that I don't like talking about my work until I've finished!"

"Stars and interstellar matter." Snegovoi repeated it slowly and shrugged. "There's the estate, and there's the water. And it's not classified? Any part of it?"

"Not a letter of it."

"And you're sure you don't know Gubar?"

"I don't know any Gubar."

Snegovoi smoked in silence next to him, huge, hunched over, frightening. Then he spoke.

"Well, well, looks like there's nothing there. I'm through with you, Dmitri. Please excuse me."

"But I'm not through with you! I'd still like to know—"

"I don't have the right!" Snegovoi said in clipped words and ended the conversation.

Of course, Malianov would not have let the matter rest with that, but then he noticed something that made him bite his tongue. There was a bulge in the left pocket of Snegovoi's pants and there was a very definite gun handle peering out of the pocket. A big gun. Like a gigantic Colt .45 from the movies. And that gun killed Malianov's desire to ask any more questions. Somehow it was very clear that something was fishy and he was not the one to ask questions. And Snegovoi got up and said:

"And now, Dmitri, I'll be leaving again tomorrow."

CHAPTER 3

Excerpt 5.... lay on his back, waking up slowly. Trucks were rolling noisily outside the window, but it was quiet in the apartment. The remnants of yesterday's senseless evening were a slight buzz in his head, a metallic aftertaste in his mouth, and an unpleasant splinter in his heart or soul or wherever the hell it hurt. He had just begun to explore what the splinter was when there was a careful knock at the door. That must be Arnold with his keys, he guessed, and hurried to answer.

On the way to the door he noted that the kitchen was cleaned up and that the door to Bobchik's room was shut tight. She must have gotten up, done the dishes, and gone back to bed, he thought.

While he struggled with the lock there was another delicate ring of the doorbell.

"Coming, coming," he said in his sleep-hoarsened voice. "Just a minute, Arnold."

But it turned out to be someone else. A complete stranger was wiping his feet on the rubber mat. The young man was wearing jeans, a black shirt with the sleeves rolled up, and large sunglasses. Just like a Tonton Macoute. Malianov noticed that on the landing, by the elevator, there were two other Tonton Macoutes in dark glasses, but before he had time to worry about them, the first Tonton Macoute said: "From the Criminal Investigation Department," and handed Malianov a little book. Opened.

"Terrific!" thought Malianov. Everything was clear. He should have expected it. He was hurt. In his shorts he stood before the Tonton Macoute from the Criminal Investigation Department and stared dully into the book. There was a photograph, some seals and signatures, but his dazed sensations let only one pertinent fact through: "Office of the Ministry of Internal Affairs." In big letters.

"Yes, of course, come in," he mumbled. "Come in."

"Thank you," said the Tonton Macoute with extreme politeness. "Are you Dmitri Alekseevich Malianov?"

"I am."

"I'd like to ask you a few questions, if you don't mind."

"Please do. Wait, my room's not made up. I just got up. Would you mind going into the kitchen? No, the sun's in there now. All right, come in here, I'll clean it up."

The Tonton Macoute went into the main room and stopped in the middle modestly, openly looking around, while Malianov straightened the bed, threw on a shirt and a pair of jeans, and opened the blinds and the window.

"Sit here, in the armchair. Or would you be more comfortable at the desk? What's the problem?"

Carefully stepping over the papers strewn on the floor, the Tonton Macoute sat in the armchair and placed his folder on his lap.

"Your passport, please."

Malianov went through the desk drawer and dug out his passport.

"Who else lives here?" the Tonton Macoute asked as he examined the passport.

"My wife, my son—but they're away now. They're in Odessa, on vacation, at her parents."

The Tonton Macoute placed the passport on top of his folder and took off his sunglasses. A fellow with a perfectly ordinary exterior. And no Tonton Macoute. A salesman, maybe. Or a television repairman.

"Let's get acquainted," he said. "I'm a senior investigator of the CID. My name is Igor Petrovich Zykov."

"My pleasure."

Then he remembered that he, damn it all, was no criminal, and that he, damn it all, was a senior scientific colleague and a Ph.D. And no boy, either, for that matter. He crossed his legs, got comfortable, and said coolly:

"I'm listening."

Zykov lifted the folder in both hands, crossed his legs, and replacing the folder on his knee, said:

"Do you know Arnold Pavlovich Snegovoi?"

Malianov was not surprised by the question. For some reason—some inexplicable reason—he knew that they would ask about either Val Weingarten or Arnold Snegovoi. And so he could answer calmly.

"Yes. I am acquainted with Colonel Snegovoi."

"And how do you know that he's a colonel?" Zykov inquired immediately.

"Well, I mean ..." Malianov avoided a direct answer. "We've known each other a long time."

"How long?"

"Well, five years, I guess. Ever since we moved into this building."

"And what were the circumstances of your meeting?"

Malianov tried to remember. What were the circumstances? Damn. When he brought the key the first time? No, we already knew each other then.

"Hm," he said, uncrossing his legs and scratching the back of his head. "You know, I don't remember. I do remember this. The elevator wasn't working, and Irina, that's my wife, was coming back from the store with groceries and the baby.

Arnold Snegovoi helped her with the packages and the boy. Well, she invited him to drop in. I think he came over that same evening."

"Was he in uniform?"

"No," Malianov said with certainty.

"So. And from that time you became friends?"

"Well, *friends* is too strong a word. He drops in sometimes—borrows books, lends books, sometimes we have a cup of tea. And when he goes away on business he leaves his keys with us."

"Why?"

"What do you mean, why? You never ..."

But actually, why did he leave the keys? It never even occurred to me to wonder. I guess, just in case, probably.

"Just in case, probably," Malianov said. "Maybe his relatives might show up—or someone else."

"Did anyone ever come?"

"No ... not that I remember. No one when I was around. Maybe my wife might know something about this."

Igor Zykov nodded thoughtfully, then asked:

"Well, have you ever talked about science, your work?"

Work again.

"Whose work?" Malianov asked darkly.

"His, of course. He was a physicist, wasn't he?"

"Haven't the slightest idea. I thought he was in rocketry."

He hadn't finished the sentence when he broke out in a sweat. What did he mean, *was*? Why the past tense? He didn't leave his key. God, what had happened? He was ready to scream at the top of his lungs, "What do you mean *was*?" but Zykov knocked him for a loop. With the swift movement of a fencer he shot his arm out and grabbed a notebook out from under Malianov's nose.

"Where did you get this?" he demanded, his face suddenly looking older. "Where did you get it?"

"Just a—"

"Sit down!" Zykov shouted. His blue eyes ran over Malianov's face. "How did this data get in your hands?"

"What data?" Malianov whispered. "What the hell data are you talking about?" he roared. "That's my calculations."

"That is not your calculations," Zykov answered coldly, also raising his voice. "Where did this graph come from?"

He showed him the page from afar and pointed to a crooked line.

"From my head!" Malianov shouted. "Right from here!" He struck his temple with his fist. "That is the relation of the density to the distance from the star!"

"This is the graph of the growth of crime in our district for the last quarter!" Zykov announced.

Malianov was dumbfounded. And Zykov, flapping his lips wetly, went on.

"You didn't even copy it right. It's not really like that, it goes this way." He picked up Malianov's pencil, jumped up, put the paper on the table, and, pressing heavily with the pencil, drew another line over Malianov's chart. "There. And over here it goes like this, not like that." When he was finished, and the pencil point was broken, he threw away the pencil, sat down again, and looked at Malianov with pity. "Eh, Malianov, Malianov. You're a highly educated man, an experienced criminal, but you behave like the lowliest punk."

Malianov kept looking back and forth from his face to the graph. It didn't make any sense at all. It was so ridiculous that it was pointless to say anything, or scream, or say nothing. Actually, the best thing to do in this case would be to wake up.

"And is your wife on good terms with Snegovoi?" Zykov asked, once again polite to the point of colorlessness.

"Good terms, yes."

"Do they use the informal *you*?"

"Listen. You've ruined my graph. What's going on?"

"What graph?" Zykov was surprised.

"This one, right here."

"That's of no consequence. Does Snegovoi drop over when you're not home?"

"Of no consequence," Malianov repeated. "It may be of no consequence to you," he said rapidly, gathering his papers and stuffing them into the drawers. "You sit here and work and kill yourself like a damn fool and then anyone who wants to comes around and tells you it's of no consequence," he muttered, getting down on all fours and gathering the rough drafts scattered on the floor.

Igor Zykov watched him expressionlessly, neatly screwing his cigarette in the holder. When Malianov, huffing, sweaty, and angry, got back to his chair, Zykov asked politely:

"May I smoke?"

"Go ahead. There's the ashtray. And get on with your questions. I have work to do."

"It all depends on you," Zykov maintained, delicately letting smoke escape from the corner of his mouth. "For example, here's a question: What do you usually call Snegovoi—Colonel, Snegovoi, or Arnold?"

"Depends. What's the difference what I call him?"

"You call him colonel?"

"Well, yes. So?"

"That's very strange," Zykov said, carefully flicking his ash. "You see, Snegovoi was promoted to colonel only the day before yesterday."

That was a shock. Malianov said nothing, feeling his face turn red.

"So how did you find out he was made colonel?"

Malianov waved his hand.

"All right. I was bragging. I didn't know he was a colonel,

or lieutenant colonel, or whatever. I dropped in on him yesterday and saw his tunic with the epaulets. And I saw he was a colonel."

"When were you there yesterday?"

"Last night. Late. I got a book. This one."

That was a mistake, mentioning the book. Zykov grabbed the book and started leafing through it. Malianov began sweating again because he didn't have the slightest idea what was in it.

"What language is this?" Zykov asked distractedly.

"Er ..." Malianov mumbled, sweating for a third time. "I would imagine English."

"I don't think so," Zykov said, peering into the text. "It looks like Cyrillic to me, not Latin. Oh! It's Russian!"

Malianov broke out in a sweat for a fourth time, but Zykov merely replaced the book, put on his dark glasses, leaned back in the armchair, and stared at Malianov. And Malianov stared at Zykov, trying not to blink or to look away. A thought ran through his mind: You son of a bitch. I won't tell you where our boys are.

"Who do you think I look like?" Zykov suddenly asked.

"Like a Tonton Macoute!" Malianov blurted without thinking.

"Wrong," Zykov said. "Try again."

"I don't know."

Zykov took off his glasses and shook his head accusingly.

"That's bad! It won't do! You have strange ideas about our investigatory organizations. How on earth did you come up with that—Tonton Macoute?"

"Well then, who do you look like?" Malianov asked, faltering.

Igor Zykov waved his sunglasses under Malianov's nose as though giving the whole thing away.

"The Invisible Man! The only thing in common with Ton-ton Macoute—the only one—is that they're both capitalized!"

He fell silent. There was a thick, heavy silence in the air; even the cars outside stopped making noise. Malianov couldn't hear a single sound, and he desperately wanted to wake up. And then the silence was shattered by the telephone.

Malianov jumped. It seemed that Zykov did, too. The phone rang again. Leaning on his forearms, Malianov raised himself up and glanced questioningly at Zykov.

"Yes. It's probably for you."

Malianov climbed over to the bed and picked up the phone. It was Val Weingarten.

"Hey, stargazer," he said. "Why don't you call, you pig?"

"You know how it is . . . I was busy."

"Fooling around with the broad?"

"No—what do you mean, 'with the broad'?"

"I wish my Svetlana would force her girlfriends on me!"

"Y-yes . . ." He felt eyes on the back of his head. "Listen, Val, I'll call you back later."

"What's wrong over there?" Weingarten demanded anxiously.

"Nothing. I'll tell you later."

"Is it that broad?"

"No."

"A man?"

"Uh-hum."

Weingarten sighed into the phone.

"Listen," he said, lowering his voice. "I can come right over. Do you want me to?"

"No! That's all I need."

Weingarten sighed heavily.

"Listen, does he have red hair?"

Malianov glanced over involuntarily at Zykov. To his

surprise, Zykov wasn't looking at him at all. He was reading Snegovoi's book, his lips moving.

"Of course not! What kind of nonsense is that? Look, I'll call you later."

"Definitely call!" Val yelled. "As soon as he leaves, call me."

"All right," Malianov said and hung up. Then he returned to his chair, mumbling excuses.

"It's all right," Zykov said and put down the book. "You have wide-ranging interests, Dmitri."

"I can't complain," Malianov muttered. Damn, I wish I could get at least one look at that book. "Please," he said placatingly, "let's finish up, if it's at all possible. It's after one already."

"Naturally!" Zykov proclaimed helpfully. He glanced at his watch anxiously and pulled out a notebook from his folder. "All right, so last night you were at Snegovoi's, correct?"

"Yes."

"For this book?"

"Y-yes," Malianov said, deciding not to clarify anything.

"When was this?"

"Late, around midnight."

"Did you have the impression that Snegovoi was planning a trip?"

"Yes, I did. I mean it wasn't an impression. He told me that he was leaving in the morning and would bring me the keys."

"Did he?"

"No. I mean, he might have rung the bell and I didn't hear him. I was sleeping."

Zykov wrote quickly, leaning the pad on the folder that lay on his knee. He did not look at Malianov at all, even when he addressed the questions at him. In a rush, perhaps?

"Did Snegovoi mention where he was going?"

"No, he never told me where he went."

"But you guessed?"

"Well, I think I had an idea. To a proving ground, or something like that."

"Did he tell you anything about it?"

"No, of course not. We never spoke about his work."

"Then what do you base your guess on?"

Malianov shrugged. What did he base it on? It's impossible to explain things like that. It was clear that the man worked in a deep bunker, his face and hands were all burned, and he had a manner that corresponded to that kind of work ... and the fact that he refused to discuss his work.

"I don't know. I just always thought so. I don't know."

"Did he introduce you to any of his friends?"

"No, never."

"His wife?"

"Is he married? I always thought he was a bachelor or a widower."

"Why did you think so?"

"I don't know," Malianov said angrily. "Intuition."

"Perhaps your wife told you so?"

"Irina? How would she know?"

"That's what I would like to clear up."

They stared at each other in silence.

"I don't understand," Malianov said. "What is it you want to clear up?"

"How your wife knew that Snegovoi wasn't married."

"Ah ... she knew that?"

Zykov did not reply. He was staring intently at Malianov and his pupils dilated and contracted ominously. Malianov was on edge. He thought he would start banging his fist on the wall, drooling, and losing face if it lasted one more second. He couldn't stand it anymore. This whole conversation had some evil subtext, it was all like a sticky web, and for some reason Irina was being dragged into it.

"Well, all right," Zykov said suddenly, shutting the note pad with a snap. "So the cognac is here," he pointed at the bar, "and the vodka is in the refrigerator. Which do you prefer? Personally?"

"Me?"

"Yes. You. Personally."

"Cognac," Malianov said hoarsely and swallowed. His throat was dry.

"Wonderful!" Zykov said cheerfully; he stood up and walked with small steps over to the bar. "We won't have far to go! Here we go," he said digging through the bar. "Ah, you even have some lemon—a little dry, but all right. Which glasses? Let's use these blue ones."

Malianov watched listlessly as Zykov deftly set up the glasses on the table, sliced the lemon thin, and uncorked the bottle.

"You know, speaking frankly, you're in bad shape. Naturally it's all up to the courts, but I've been at this for ten years, and I have some experience in these matters. And you can always guess what sentence each case will get. You won't get the maximum, of course, but I can guarantee you fifteen, at least." He poured the cognac carefully into the glasses without spilling a drop. "Of course, there may always be mitigating circumstances, but for now, frankly, I don't see any—I just don't see any, Dmitri! Well!" He raised his glass and nodded invitingly.

Malianov took his glass with numb fingers.

"All right," he said in a voice that was not his own. "But could I at least know what's going on?"

"Naturally!" Zykov shrieked. He drank his glass, popped a piece of lemon into his mouth, and nodded energetically. "Of course you can! I'll tell you everything. I have every right to do so."

And he told him.

At eight o'clock that morning a car came to pick up Snegovoi and take him to the airport. To the driver's surprise, Snegovoi was not waiting downstairs as usual. He waited five minutes and then went up to the apartment. No one answered even though the bell was working—the driver could hear it himself. So he went downstairs and called the office from the corner. The company began calling Snegovoi on the phone. Snegovoi's phone was constantly busy. Meanwhile, the driver walked around the house and discovered that all three windows in Snegovoi's apartment were wide open and, in spite of the daylight, all the electric lights were on. The driver phoned with the information. The right people were called in, and they broke down the door and examined Snegovoi's apartment. Their investigation revealed that all the lamps in the apartment were on, that an open, packed suitcase stood on the bed, and that Snegovoi was at his desk in his study, holding the phone in one hand and a Makarov pistol in the other. It was determined that Snegovoi had died of a bullet wound to the right temple fired at point-blank range from that gun. Death was instantaneous and took place between three and four a.m.

"What does that have to do with me?" Malianov whispered.

In reply Zykov told him in detail how ballistics had plotted the trajectory of the bullet and found it lodged in the wall.

"But what does that have to do with me?" Malianov kept asking, thumping himself on the chest. They had already had three shots each.

"Aren't you sorry for him?" Zykov asked. "Do you feel sorry for him?"

"Of course I do. He was an excellent man. But what do I have to do with this? I've never had a gun in my hand in my whole life; I was rejected by the army. My eyesight . . ."

Zykov wasn't listening to him. He kept explaining in detail that the deceased had been left-handed and that it was very strange that he shot himself with the gun in his right hand.

"Yes, yes, Arnold was left-handed, I can corroborate that. But as for me! I slept all night! And anyway, why would I kill him? Judge for yourself!"

"Then who did? Who?" Zykov asked gently.

"How should I know? You should know who!"

"You!" Zykov said in an ingratiating tone reminiscent of Porfiry in *Crime and Punishment*, peering with one eye at Malianov over his vodka glass. "*You* killed him, Dmitri!"

"This is a nightmare," Malianov muttered helplessly. He wanted to cry.

A light breeze crossed the room, moving the blind, and the strident midday sun rushed into the room and hit Zykov smack in the face. He squinted, shielded his face with his hand, moved in his chair, and quickly set the glass on the table. Something happened to him. His eyes blinked rapidly, color came to his cheeks, and his chin quivered.

"Forgive me," he whispered in a completely human voice. "Forgive me, Dmitri. Perhaps you could ... it's very ... in here."

He stopped because something fell in Bobchik's room and shattered with a resounding noise.

"What was that?" Zykov asked, tensely. There was no more trace of human quality in his voice.

"There's someone there," Malianov said, still not understanding what had happened to Zykov. A new thought came to him. "Listen!" he shouted, jumping up. "Come with me! My wife's girlfriend is in there! She can vouch that I slept all night and didn't go anywhere."

Shoulders bumping, they jostled their way into the foyer.

"Interesting, very interesting," Zykov was saying. "Your wife's girlfriend. We'll see."

"She'll vouch for me. You'll see. She's a witness."

They rushed into Bobchik's room without knocking and stopped. The room was cleaned up and empty. There was no Lidochka in there, no sheets on the bed, no suitcase. And sitting on the floor next to the pieces of the clay pitcher (Khorezm, eleventh century) sat Kaliam with an unbelievably innocent air.

"This?" Zykov asked, pointing at Kaliam.

"No," Malianov answered stupidly. "This is our cat, we've had him a long time. But wait, where's Lidochka?" He looked in the closet. Her white jacket was gone. "She must have left?"

Zykov shrugged.

"Probably. She's not here now."

Stepping heavily, Malianov went over to the broken pitcher. "B-bastard!" he said and cuffed Kaliam's ear.

Kaliam beat a hasty retreat. Malianov crouched. Shattered. What a beautiful pitcher it had been.

"Did she sleep here?" Zykov asked.

"Yes."

"When did you see her last? Today?"

Malianov shook his head.

"Yesterday. Well, actually today. In the night. I gave her sheets and a blanket." He looked into Bobchik's linen trunk. "There. It's all there."

"Has she been living here long?"

"She arrived yesterday."

"Are her things here?"

"I don't see any. And her coat is gone."

"Strange, isn't it?" Zykov said.

Malianov just waved his hand in silence.

"The hell with her. Women are nothing but trouble. Let's have another shot."

Suddenly the front door swung open, and in walked ...

Excerpt 6. . . . elevator door, and the motor hummed. Malianov was alone.

He stood in the doorway to Bobchik's room leaning on the frame and thinking about nothing. Kaliam appeared out of nowhere, walking past him, tail twitching, and went out onto the landing, where he set about licking the cement floor.

"Well, all right," Malianov said finally, then tore himself away from the door frame and went into his room. It was smoke-filled and three blue glasses stood abandoned on the table—two empty and one half full. The sun was up to the bookshelves.

"He took the cognac with him! That's all I need!"

He sat in the armchair for a while, finished his glass. Noises from the street came in through the window, and the open door let in children's voices and elevator grumblings from the stairs. He got up, dragged himself through the foyer, bumping into the doorjamb, plodded out onto the landing, and stopped in front of Snegovoi's apartment door. There was a big wax seal on the lock. He touched it gingerly with a fingertip and pulled his hand away. It was all true. Everything that had happened had really happened. Citizen of the Soviet Union Arnold Snegovoi, colonel and man of mystery, was no more.

CHAPTER 4

Excerpt 7.... washed the glasses and put them away, cleaned up the pieces in Bobchik's room, and gave Kaliam some fish. Then he took down Bobchik's milk glass, put three raw eggs into it, added pieces of bread, heavily salted and peppered the mixture, and stirred. He wasn't hungry; he was functioning on automatic pilot. And he ate the glop, standing by the balcony window watching the sun-flooded empty courtyard. Couldn't they plant some trees? Even one?

His thoughts moved on in a feeble trickle, not really thoughts, just bits and pieces. Maybe these are the new investigative methods, he thought. The scientific and technological revolution and all that. Free and easy behavior and psychological attack. But the cognac, that was completely unclear. Igor Petrovich Zykov. Or was it Zykin? Well, anyway, that was what he said his name was, but what did it say in his documents? Those con men! he thought suddenly. They pulled that whole prank just for a lousy half bottle of cognac?

No, Snegovoi had died. That was clear. I'll never see Snegovoi again. He was a good man, but disorganized. He always seemed out of sorts, particularly yesterday. And yet he was calling somebody; he wanted to say something, explain, warn about something. Malianov shuddered. He put the dirty glass in the sink. The embryo of the future pile of dirty dishes. Lidochka sure did a good job on the kitchen, everything sparkled. He warned me about Lidochka. Really, it was very strange about Lidochka.

Malianov rushed to the foyer and looked for Irina's note. No, it was just his imagination. Everything was in order. It was obviously Irina's handwriting and her style—and anyway, why would a killer stay around to do the dishes?

Excerpt 8. . . . Val's phone was busy. Malianov hung up and stretched out on the sofa, his nose in the itchy blanket. Something was wrong at Val's house, too. Some kind of hysteria. It's happened before. A fight with Svetlana, or with his mother-in-law. What was that he asked me, something strange? Ah, Val, I should have your troubles! No, let him come over. He's hysterical; I'm hysterical—maybe the two of us can come up with a solution. Malianov dialed again, and it was still busy. Damn, what a waste of time! I should be working, but there's all this mess.

Suddenly he heard someone cough behind him in the foyer. Malianov flew off the sofa. For nothing, of course. There was no one in the foyer. Or in the bathroom. He checked the lock and came back to the sofa, whereupon he realized that his knees were wobbly. Hell, my nerves are shot. And that creep kept telling me that he was like the Invisible Man. You look like a tapeworm with glasses, you creep, not the Invisible Man! Bastard. He dialed Val's number again, hung up, and began pulling on his socks with determination. I'll call from Vecherovsky's. It's my own fault that I'm wasting time. He put on a fresh shirt, checked that his keys were in his pocket, locked the door, and ran up the stairs.

On the sixth floor a couple was making out by the incinerator chute. The guy was wearing sunglasses, but Malianov knew the punk—he was an aspiring do-nothing from Apartment 17. He was in his second year of unemployment and steadily not

looking for work. He didn't run into anyone else on his way
to the eighth floor. But all the while he had the feeling that he
would bump into someone. They would grab his arm and say
softly: "Just a second, citizen."

Thank God, Phil was home. And as usual he was dressed
as if ready to leave for the Dutch Embassy for a reception for
her Royal Highness, the car would be picking him up in five
minutes. He was wearing a phenomenally gorgeous cream-
colored suit, loafers beyond mere mortal dreams, and a tie.
That tie always depressed Malianov. He just couldn't understand how anyone could work at home in a tie.

"Are you working?" Malianov asked.

"As usual."

"I won't stay long."

"Of course. Some coffee?"

"Wait. No, why not. Please."

They went to the kitchen. Malianov took a chair, and
Vecherovsky began the ritual with the coffee-making equip-
ment.

"I'll make Viennese coffee," he said without turning.

"Fine," Malianov said. "Do you have whipped cream?"

Vecherovsky did not reply. Malianov watched his protrud-
ing shoulder blades work under the creamy fabric.

"Did the criminal investigator come to see you?" Malianov
asked.

The shoulder blades stopped for a second, and then the
long, freckled face with the droopy nose and red eyebrows,
raised high over the tortoiseshell eyeglasses, appeared slowly
over his round, stooped shoulder.

"Sorry. What did you say?"

"I said: Did the criminal investigator come to see you
today?"

"Why a criminal investigator?"

"Because Snegovoi shot himself. They've already talked to me."

"Who's Snegovoi?"

"You know, the guy who lives across the hall from me. The rocketry guy."

"Oh."

Vecherovsky turned away and his shoulder blades started up again.

"Didn't you know him? I thought I had introduced you."

"No," said Vecherovsky. "Not as far as I can remember."

A marvelous coffee aroma filled the kitchen. Malianov settled comfortably into the chair. Should he tell him or not? In that aromatic kitchen, cool despite the blinding sun, where everything was in its place and everything was of top quality—the best in the world or even better—the events of the last day seemed particularly crazy and improbable, even unhealthy, somehow.

"Do you know the joke about the two roosters?" Malianov asked.

"Two roosters? I know one about three roosters. A terrible joke."

"No, no. It's about two roosters," Malianov said. "You don't know it?"

And he told the joke about the two roosters. Vecherovsky did not react at all. One would have thought that he was faced with a serious problem instead of a joke—he was so serious and thoughtful when he set the cup of coffee and the creamer in front of Malianov. Then he poured himself a cup and sat down across the table, holding the cup in the air, taking a sip, and finally pronouncing:

"Excellent. Not your joke. I mean the coffee."

"I got it," Malianov said glumly.

They silently enjoyed the Viennese coffee. Then Vecherovsky broke the silence.

"I thought about your problem some yesterday. Have you tried Hartwig's function?"

"I know, I know. I figured that out for myself."

Malianov pushed away the empty cup.

"Listen, Phil. I can't think about the damn function! My brain is in a muddle, and you . . ."

Excerpt 9. . . . nothing for a minute, rubbing his smooth-shaved cheek with two fingers, and then declaimed:

"We could not look death in the face, they bound our eyes and brought us to her." Then he added, "Poor guy."

It wasn't clear who he had in mind.

"I mean, I can understand everything," Malianov said. "But that investigator . . ."

"Want some more coffee?" Vecherovsky interrupted.

Malianov shook his head, and Vecherovsky stood up.

"Then let's go into my room," he said.

They moved to his studio. Vecherovsky sat down at his desk, completely bare except for one single piece of paper right in the middle, took a mechanical phone directory from the drawer, pushed a button, read down the page, and dialed the phone number.

"Senior Investigator Zykin, please," he said in a dry, businesslike voice. "I mean, Zykov, Igor Petrovich. Out on operations? Thank you." He hung up. "Senior Investigator Zykov is out on operations," he told Malianov.

"He's out drinking my cognac with some girls, that's what he's out doing," grumbled Malianov.

Vecherovsky bit his lip.

"That doesn't matter. The point is he exists!"

"Of course he exists! He showed me his papers. Why, did you think they were crooks?"

"I doubt it."

"That's what I thought. To do that whole story just for a bottle of cognac, and right next door to a sealed apartment."

Vecherovsky nodded.

"And you say—Hartwig's function! How can I work at a time like this? There's enough going on."

Vecherovsky looked at him intently.

"Dmitri," he said. "Didn't it surprise you that Snegovoi took an interest in your work?"

"And how! We'd never talked about work before."

"And what did you tell him?"

"Well, in very general terms—in fact, he didn't insist on details."

"And what did he say?"

"Nothing. I think he was disappointed. He said, 'There's the estate, and there's the water.'"

"What?"

"'There's the estate, and there's the water.'"

"And what is that supposed to mean?"

"It's a literary reference. You know, that you ask about the rope, and you get an answer about the sky."

"Aha." Vecherovsky blinked with his bovine lashes, then took a pristine, sparkling ashtray from the windowsill and a pipe and tobacco pouch and began filling the pipe. "Aha ... 'there's the estate, and there's the water.' ... I like that. I'll have to remember it."

Malianov waited impatiently. He had great faith in him. Vecherovsky had a totally inhuman brain. Malianov knew no one else who could come up with such completely unexpected conclusions.

"Well?" he finally demanded.

Vecherovsky had filled his pipe and was now slowly smoking and savoring it. The pipe made little wheezing sounds. Inhaling, Vecherovsky said:

"Dmitri ... pf-pf-pf ... how much have you moved along since Thursday? I think Thursday ... pf-pf ... was the last time we talked."

"What difference does it make?" Malianov asked, annoyed. "I don't have time for that now."

Vecherovsky let those words go right by him. He kept looking at Malianov with his reddish eyes and puffed on his pipe. That was Vecherovsky. He had asked a question, and now he was waiting for an answer. Malianov gave up. He believed that Vecherovsky knew better than he what was important and what wasn't.

"I've moved along considerably," he said, and began describing how he reformulated the problem and reduced it to an equation in vector form and then to an integral-differential equation, how he began getting a physical picture of it, how he figured out the M cavities, and how last night he finally figured out that he should use Hartwig's transformation.

Vecherovsky listened attentively, without interrupting or asking questions, and only once, when Malianov got carried away, grabbed the solitary piece of paper, and tried to write on the back of it, he stopped him and said, "In words, in words."

"But I didn't have time to act on any of it," Malianov wound up sadly. "Because first the crazy phone calls began, and then the guy from the store came over."

"You didn't tell me about any of this," Vecherovsky interrupted.

"Well, it has nothing to do with it," Malianov replied. "I could still get some work done with all the telephone calls, but then that Lidochka showed up, and it all went to hell ..."

Vecherovsky was completely enveloped in puffs and plumes of honeyed smoke.

"Not bad, not bad," his soft voice said. "But you stopped, I see, at the most interesting spot."

"I didn't stop, I was stopped!"

"Yes," said Vecherovsky.

Malianov struck his knees with his fists. "Damn, I could be doing so much work right now! But I can't think! Every rustle in my own apartment makes me jump like a psycho ... and then there's that lovely prospect—fifteen years in prison camp ..."

He brought up the fifteen years yet again, always waiting for Vecherovsky to say "Stop imagining things, that won't happen, don't even think about it ..." But this time, too, Vecherovsky said nothing of the kind. Instead, he started questioning Malianov at length and in detail about the phone calls: when did they start (exactly), where were they calling (well, just a few concrete examples), who called (man? woman? child?) When Malianov told him about the calls from Weingarten, he seemed surprised and kept silent for a while, and then went back to his questions. What did Malianov say when he picked up? Did he always pick up? What did they tell him at the telephone repair service? By the way, it was only then that Malianov recalled that after his second call to the repair service that the wrong numbers stopped ... But he didn't have time to tell Vecherovsky about it because he remembered something else.

"Listen," he said, becoming excited. "I completely forgot. Weingarten, when he called yesterday, wanted to know if I knew Snegovoi."

"Yes?"

"Yes. I said that I did."

"And he said?"

"And he said that he didn't know him. But that's not the point. What do you think, is it a coincidence? Or what? It's a strange coincidence."

Vecherovsky said nothing, puffing on his pipe. Then he went back to his questions. What was the story with the delivery? More detail. What did the guy look like? What did he say? What did he bring? What's left of the delivery? The monotonous questioning depressed Malianov completely because he couldn't understand what any of it had to do with his bad luck. Then Vecherovsky finally shut up and poked around in his pipe. Malianov waited and then began imagining how four men would come for him, all in black sunglasses, and how they would search the apartment, pulling off the wallpaper and demanding to know if he'd had relations with Lidochka, and not believing him, and then taking him away.

"What's going to happen to me?"

Vecherovsky answered.

"Who knows what's in store for us? Who knows what will be? The strong will be, and the blackguards will be. And death will come and sentence you to death. Do not pursue the future . . ."

Malianov realized this was poetry only because Vecherovsky lapsed into muffled guffaws that passed for satisfied laughter. That's probably the sound H. G. Wells's Martians made when they drank human blood; Vecherovsky guffawed like that because he liked the poem he had just read. One would think that the pleasure he derived from poetry was purely physical.

"Go to hell," Malianov said.

And that prompted a second tirade—a prose one this time.

"When I feel bad, I work," Vecherovsky said. "When I have problems, when I'm depressed, when I'm bored with life, I sit down to my work. There are probably other prescriptions, but I don't know them. Or they don't work for me. You want my advice—here it is: Go and work. Thank God that people like you and me need only paper and pencil to work."

Say that Malianov knew all that without him. From books. But it wasn't that simple for Malianov. He could work only when he felt lighthearted and there was nothing hanging over him.

"Some help you are," he said. "Let me call Weingarten. I'm still puzzled why he asked about Snegovoi."

"Sure," said Vecherovsky. "But if you don't mind, move the phone into the other room."

Malianov took the phone and dragged the wire into the next room.

"If you want, stay here," Vecherovsky called after him. "I have paper and I'll give you a pencil."

"All right, we'll see."

Now Weingarten didn't answer. Malianov let it ring ten times, then dialed again and let it ring ten more. What should he do now? Of course, he could stay here. It was cool and quiet. All the rooms were air-conditioned. He couldn't hear the trucks and squealing brakes because the apartment faced the courtyard. And then he realized that that wasn't the issue. He was simply afraid to go back to his own apartment. That does it! I love my home more than anything else in the world, and now I'm afraid to go back there? Oh, no. You won't get me to do that. Sorry, but no way.

Malianov picked up the phone firmly and brought it back. Vecherovsky was sitting staring into the one piece of paper, quietly drumming on it with his expensive pen. The page was half covered with symbols that Malianov couldn't understand.

"I'm going, Phil," Malianov said.

Vecherovsky looked up at him.

"Of course. I have to administer an exam tomorrow, but I'll be home all day today. Call me or drop by."

"All right."

He went downstairs slowly; there was no rush. I'll brew up a cup of strong tea, sit in the kitchen; Kaliam will climb up into my lap; I'll pet him, sip my tea, and try to sort this out calmly and soberly. Too bad we don't have a TV; it would be nice to spend the evening in front of the box watching something mindless, like a comedy or some soccer. I'll play solitaire; I haven't done that in ages.

He came down to his landing, found his keys, turned the corner, and stopped. His heart had sunk somewhere into the vicinity of his stomach and was beating slowly and rhythmically, like a pile driver. The door to his apartment was open.

He tiptoed up to the door and listened. There was someone in the apartment. He could hear an unfamiliar man's voice and a response in an unfamiliar child's voice . . .

CHAPTER 5

Excerpt 10. . . . strange man was crouching on the floor and picking up the pieces of a broken glass. There was also a boy of five or so in the kitchen. He was sitting on the stool, his hands under his thighs, swinging his legs and watching the man pick up the pieces.

"Listen, buddy," Weingarten shouted when he saw Malianov, "where did you disappear to?"

His huge cheeks were ablaze with a purple glow, his olive-black eyes were shining, and his thick tar-black hair was disheveled. It was apparent that he had had quite a few already. A half-empty bottle of export Stolichnaya stood on the table amid all kinds of goodies from the delivery crate.

"Relax and take it easy," Weingarten continued. "We didn't touch the caviar. We were waiting for you."

The man picking up the pieces stood. He was a tall, handsome man with a Viking beard and the beginnings of a potbelly. He smiled in embarrassment.

"Well, well, well!" Malianov said, entering the kitchen and feeling his heart rise from his stomach and return to its proper place. "I believe the expression is 'my home is my castle'?"

"Taken by storm, old buddy, taken by storm!" Weingarten shouted. "Listen, where did you get such good vodka? And those eats?"

Malianov extended his hand to the handsome stranger,

and he extended his, but it was full of broken glass. There was a small, pleasant moment of discomfort.

"We've been helping ourselves here," he said with embarrassment. "I'm afraid it's all my fault."

"Nonsense, here, throw that in the garbage."

"Mister is a coward," the boy said clearly.

Malianov shuddered. And it looked as if the others did too.

"Sh, sh," the handsome man said, and waved his finger at the boy in warning.

"Child!" Weingarten said. "You were given some chocolate, I believe. Well, sit there quietly and chomp on it. And do not add your two cents' worth."

"Why do you say I'm a coward?" said Malianov, sitting down. "Why do you insult me?"

"I'm not insulting you," the boy said, observing him as though he were a rare specimen in the wild. "I was just describing you."

Meanwhile the stranger got rid of the glass, wiped his hand with his handkerchief, and extended his hand.

"Zakhar," he introduced himself.

They shook hands ceremoniously.

"To business!" Weingarten bustled, rubbing his hands together. "Get two more glasses."

"Listen, fellows, I'm not drinking any vodka," Malianov said.

"Then we'll drink some wine," Weingarten concurred. "You still have two bottles of white left."

"No, I think I'll have some cognac. Zakhar, would you be so kind as to get the caviar and butter from the refrigerator ... and everything else. I'm starving."

Malianov went over to the bar, got the cognac and glasses, stuck his tongue out at the chair that had been occupied by the Tonton Macoute, and came back to the table. The table was groaning under the spread. I'll eat my fill and get drunk, thought Malianov. I'm glad the guys came over.

But nothing went the way he had planned. No sooner had he finished his drink and settled down to eating a piece of bread spread thick with caviar than Weingarten said in a completely sober voice:

"And now, buddy, tell us what happened to you."

Malianov choked.

"What are you talking about?"

"Look," Weingarten said. "There are three of us here, and each of us has had a run-in. So don't be embarrassed. What did the red-haired guy say to you?"

"Vecherovsky?"

"No, no, what does Vecherovsky have to do with it? You were visited by a tiny man with flaming red hair, wearing a deathly black outfit. What did he tell you?"

Malianov bit off a piece that filled up his whole mouth and chewed without tasting it. All three stared at him. Zakhar looked at him in embarrassment, smiling meekly, even glancing away from time to time. Weingarten's eyes were bulging and he looked ready to start shouting at the drop of a pin. And the boy, hanging on to his melting chocolate, was staring intently at Malianov.

"Fellows," Malianov finally said. "What red-haired man are you talking about? Nobody like that came to visit me. My visitors were a lot worse."

"Well, tell us," Weingarten said impatiently.

"Why should I tell you?" Malianov was incensed. "I'm not making a secret out of it, but what are you trying to pull here? Tell me first! And by the way, I'd like to know how you found out that anything had happened to me in the first place!"

"You tell me and then I'll tell you," Weingarten insisted stubbornly. "And Zakhar will tell his."

"You both tell first," Malianov said nervously, making himself another sandwich. "There's two of you against one of me."

"You tell," the boy commanded, pointing at Malianov.

"Sh, sh," Zakhar whispered, completely embarrassed.

Weingarten laughed sadly.

"Is he yours?" Malianov asked Zakhar.

"Sort of," Zakhar answered strangely, looking away.

"His, he's his," Weingarten said impatiently. "By the way, that's part of his story. Well, Dmitri, come on, don't be shy."

They confused Malianov utterly. He put his sandwich aside and started talking. From the very beginning, from the phone calls. When you tell the same horrible story twice in the space of two hours, you begin to find its amusing side. Malianov hadn't even noticed how he was going at it. Weingarten began giggling, revealing his powerful, yellowish eyeteeth, and Malianov seemed to have made it his life's work to get a laugh from Zakhar, but he never did manage it. Zakhar smiled distractedly and almost pityingly. But when Malianov got to the part about Snegovoi's suicide, it wasn't a laughing matter anymore.

"You're lying!" Weingarten said hoarsely.

Malianov shrugged. "If you want to think so, that's your prerogative," he said. "But his door has been sealed, you can go and see for yourself."

Weingarten sat in silence for some time, drumming his fingers on the table, his cheeks quivering in rhythm, and then he got up noisily, looking at no one, squeezed between Zakhar and the boy, and stomped away. They could hear the lock smack open; the smell of cabbage soup wafted into the apartment.

"Oho, ho-ho-ho," Zakhar muttered glumly.

The boy immediately offered him the messy chocolate bar, demanding:

"Take a bite!"

Zakhar obediently took a bite and chewed it. The door slammed and Weingarten, still avoiding looking at any of them, squeezed back to his chair, gulped down a shot of vodka, and said hoarsely:

"And then?"

"There's no more. Then I went up to Vecherovsky's. The creeps left, and I went up there. I just got back."

"And the redhead?" Weingarten asked impatiently.

"I told you, you blockhead! There was no redhead!"

Weingarten and Zakhar looked at each other.

"All right, we'll assume that's the truth," said Weingarten. "That girl, Lidochka. Did she make any offers?"

"Well, I mean," Malianov laughed nervously, "I mean, if I had wanted to, I could have."

"Jeez, you jerk! I don't mean that. All right, what about the investigator?"

"You know, Val, I've told you everything, just as it happened. Go to hell! I swear, a third grilling in one day!"

"Val," said Zakhar indecisively, "maybe this really was something different?"

"Don't be a fool! How could it be something else? He has work; they don't let him do it. What else could it be? And besides, his name was mentioned."

"Who mentioned my name?" Malianov asked, with a sense of foreboding.

"I have to pee," the boy announced in clear bell-like tones.

They all looked at him. He examined them one by one, climbed off the stool, and said to Zakhar:

"Let's go."

Zakhar smiled sheepishly, said, "Well, let's go," and they disappeared behind the bathroom door. They chased Kaliam off the toilet seat.

"Who mentioned my name?" Malianov asked Weingarten. "What's all this about?"

Weingarten, head bent, was listening to what went on in the toilet.

"Hell, Gubar's really gotten stuck," he said with some sort of sad satisfaction. "Really stuck!"

Something churned slowly in Malianov's brain.

"Gubar?"

"Yeah. Zakhar Gubar. You know, even twisting someone around your finger ..."

Malianov remembered. "Is he in rocketry?"

"Who? Zakhar?" Weingarten was surprised. "No, I doubt it. He's a master craftsman. Though he does work in some closed place."

"He's not military?"

"Well, you know, all those places are to some degree ..."

"I'm asking about Gubar."

"No. He's a techie, with magic hands. Makes computerized fleas. But that's not the problem. The problem is that he is a man who approaches his desires with care and thoroughness. Those are his very words. And, buddy, it's the truth."

The boy returned to the kitchen and climbed back onto the stool. Zakhar walked in after him.

"Zakhar, you know, I just remembered. Snegovoi asked about you."

And Malianov saw for the first time in his life just how a person turns white before your very eyes. Turns as white as a sheet.

"About me?" Zakhar mouthed.

"Yes. Last night." Malianov hadn't expected a reaction like that.

"Did you know him?" Weingarten asked Zakhar softly.

Zakhar shook his head silently, fished for a cigarette,

spilled half the pack on the floor, and hurriedly started picking
them up. Weingarten croaked: "Well, buddies, this is something that needs . . ." and poured some more vodka. And the
boy spoke.

"Big deal! That doesn't mean anything in itself."

Malianov shuddered again, and Zakhar sat up and looked
at the boy with something like hope.

"It's just a coincidence," the boy went on. "Look in the
phone book, there's at least eight Gubars in there."

Excerpt 11. . . . Malianov had known him since sixth grade.
They became pals in the seventh grade and shared a desk
all through school. Weingarten didn't change over the years,
he just got bigger. He was always jolly, fat, carnivorous, and
always collecting something or other—stamps, coins, post-
marks, bottle labels. Once, this was when he was already a
biologist, he decided to collect excrement because Zhenka
Sidortsev brought him whale excrement from the Antarctic
and Sanya Zhitniuk brought back some human excrement
from Penjekent, not regular of course, but fossilized, from
the ninth century. He was always bugging his friends to show
him their change—looking for a special copper coin. And
he was always grabbing your mail or begging for your post-
marked envelopes.

And with all that, he knew his business. He had been a department head in his institute for a long time, was a member
of twenty various commissions, both Soviet and international,
was always traveling abroad to all kinds of congresses, and
was just around the corner from a full professorship. He held
Vecherovsky in the highest esteem of all his friends, because
Vecherovsky was a state prize laureate, and Val dreamed of
becoming one himself. He must have told Malianov a hundred times how he would put on the medal and wear it on a

date. He was always a blowhard. He was a brilliant raconteur, and the dullest common events became dramas from Graham Greene or Le Carré in his retelling. But, strange as it seems, he lied very rarely and was horribly embarrassed when caught in one. For some unknown reason Irina did not like him. Malianov suspected that in their early years, before Bobchik was born, Weingarten made a pass at Irina, and she rejected him. Weingarten was a master at making out, not that he was a sex fiend or a degenerate—no, he was joyful, energetic, and as prepared for defeat as for victory. Every date was an adventure, no matter what its outcome. His wife, Sveta, an unbelievably beautiful woman, but subject to depression, had accepted his womanizing a long time ago, particularly since he doted upon her and was always getting into fights over her in public places. He liked brawling in general—it was a masochistic act to enter a restaurant in his company. In short, he had lived a smooth, happy, and successful life without any major upheavals.

Strange things began happening to him, it turned out, some two weeks before, when the series of experiments begun the previous year suddenly started yielding completely unexpected, and even sensational, results. ("You, old buddies, wouldn't be able to understand, it has to do with reverse transcriptase—it is RNA-dependent DNA polymerase, that's an enzyme in the makeup of oncornaviruses, and that, I can tell you right off, buddies, smells like the Nobel Prize to me.") In his labs no one other than Weingarten himself appreciated the results. Most of them, the way it usually is, didn't give a damn, and other creative individuals simply decided that the series of tests was a failure. Since it was summer, everyone was impatient to go on vacation. Weingarten wouldn't sign anyone's leave papers. There was an uproar—hurt feelings, local grievance committee, the Party bureau meeting. And in the heat of the battle, at one of the hearings, Weingarten was

semiofficially informed that there was a plan afoot to name
Comrade Valentin Andreevich Weingarten as director of the
newest, supermodern biological center then under construc-
tion in Dobroliubov.

This information made Comrade Weingarten's head spin,
but he nevertheless realized that the directorship was, first of
all, just a bird in the bush, and if and when it became a bird
in the hand it would, secondly, get V. A. Weingarten out of
creative lab work for at least a year and a half, maybe two. And
meanwhile the Nobel Prize was the Nobel Prize, buddies.

Therefore Weingarten simply promised to think it over
and went back to his lab and the mysterious reverse transcriptase and the unending brouhaha. Just two days later he was
called into the chief academician's office and quizzed about
his current project. ("I kept a tight lock on my lips, buddies, I
was extremely controlled.") It was suggested that he drop this
questionable nonsense and take up the problem of such and
such, which was of great economic significance, and therefore promising great material and spiritual rewards, which the
chief academician was willing to bet his own head on.

Flabbergasted by all these vistas suddenly yawning before him for no reason at all, Weingarten made the mistake
of bragging about them at home, and not simply at home, but
in front of his mother-in-law, whom he calls Cap because she
really was a captain second class retired. And the sky dark-
ened above his head. ("Buddies, from that evening on, my
house turned into a sawmill. They sawed at me night and day,
demanding that I accept immediately, and accept both offers
at that.")

Meanwhile, the lab, despite the occasional turmoil, continued to produce a heap of results, one more amazing than
the next. Then his aunt died, a distant relative on his father's
side, and while clearing up the estate, Weingarten discovered a

chest in the attic of her house in Kavgolova stuffed with Soviet coins out of circulation since 1961. You have to know Weingarten to believe this, but as soon as he found the chest, he lost all interest in everything else, up to and including his languishing Nobel Prize. He holed up at home and spent four days poring over the contents of the chest, deaf to the phone calls from the institute and to his mother-in-law's nagging speeches. He found fantastic specimens in that chest. Oh, luxury! But that was not the point.

When he was through with this chest and came back to work, he saw that the discovery was, so to speak, discovered. Of course, there was much that was unclear and it all had to be formulated—no mean feat, by the way—but there could be no more doubt: He had made his discovery. Weingarten started working like a squirrel on a wheel. He put an end to the squabbles at the lab ("Buddies, I threw them all out to go to hell on their vacations!"), moved Cap and the girls out to the country in twenty-four hours, canceled all his appointments, and had just got settled down at home to do the finishing strokes, when came the day before yesterday.

The day before yesterday, just as Weingarten started to work, that redhead showed up at the apartment—a short, coppery fellow with a very pale face, encased in a buttoned-up black coat of ancient cut and style. He came out of the children's room and, while Val just gaped at him in silence, sat on the edge of the desk and started talking. Without any preamble he announced that a certain extraterrestrial civilization had been watching him, V. A. Weingarten, for quite some time, following his scientific work with attention and anxiety. That the latest work of the aforementioned Weingarten was making them very anxious. That he, the redhead, was empowered to ask V. A. Weingarten to immediately drop the project and destroy all his papers relating to it.

There is absolutely no need for you to know why and wherefore we demand this, the red-haired man said. You should be told that we have tried other means, to make it seem completely natural. You should not be under the impression that the offered directorship, the new project, the discovery of the coins, or even the vacation incident in the labs were in any way purely accidental. We tried to stop you. However, since we were only able to hold you up, and not for long, we were forced to embark on an extreme measure, such as my visit to you. You should also know that all the offers made to you were and are valid and that you may still take them up if our demands are met. And, in case you do agree, we are willing to help satisfy your petty, and completely understandable, desires that arise from your human nature. As a token of the promise, allow me to give you this small gift.

And with those words, the redhead pulled a package out of thin air and tossed it on the desk in front of Weingarten. It turned out to contain marvelous stamps, whose value could not even be imagined by someone who was not a professional philatelist.

Weingarten, continued the red-haired man, should in no way think that he was the only earthling being watched by the supercivilization. There were at least three people among Weingarten's friends whose work was about to be nipped in the bud. He, the redhead, could name such names as Dmitri Alekseevich Malianov, astronomer; Zakhar Zakharovich Gubar, engineer; and Arnold Pavlovich Snegovoi, physicist. They were giving V. A. Weingarten three days, starting right now, to think it over, after which the supercivilization would feel that it had the right to employ the rather harsh "measures of the third degree."

"While he was telling me all of this," Weingarten said, "buddies, all I was thinking about was how he had gotten into the apartment without a key. Especially since I had the door bolted. Could he be some thief who had gotten in a long time ago and got bored hiding under the couch? Well, I'll show him, I thought. But while I was thinking all of that, the redhead finished up his little speech." Weingarten paused for effect.

"And flew out the window," Malianov said, gritting his teeth.

"That's for your flying out the window!" Weingarten, unembarrassed by the child, made an eloquent gesture. "He simply vanished!"

"Val," said Malianov.

"I'm telling you, buddy! He was sitting right in front of me on the desk. I was just about to give it to him on the kisser, without even standing up ... when he was gone! Like in the movies, you know?"

Weingarten grabbed the last piece of sturgeon and shoved it into his mouth.

"Moam?" he said. "Moam mooam?" He swallowed with difficulty and, blinking his tear-filled eyes, went on: "I'm a little calmer now, buddies, but back then, let me tell you, I leaned back in the chair, closed my eyes, and remembered his words; everything in me was quivering and shaking, like a pig's tail. I thought I was going to die right then and there. Nothing like that had ever happened to me. I somehow made it to my mother-in-law's room, grabbed her valerian drops—didn't help. Then I saw she had bromides, and I took those, too."

"Wait," Malianov said irritably. "Drop the clowning. I'm in no mood ... What really happened? But please, without the red-haired aliens!"

"Chum," Weingarten said, eyes bulging to the limit. "I'll cross myself, on my Pioneer's honor!" He made the sign of the cross, clumsily, with a Catholic accent. "I wasn't in any mood for joking myself ..."

Excerpt 12. . . . collected stamps, very energetically. Weingarten once took away with a satisfied purr the remnants of the stamp collection Malianov had as a teenager. He knew about stamps. He lost his tongue for a while. Yes, of course the royal collection had all of them. Mr. Stulov in New York had a few of these too. But if you just take the state collection . . . without even mentioning simple collectors . . .

"Counterfeit," said Malianov finally. Contemptuously, Weingarten said nothing. "Well, then, brand new."

"You fool," Weingarten barked and put away the book.

Malianov couldn't think of a comeback. If all this had been a lie or even the simple truth, rather than the horrible truth, Weingarten would have done it just the other way around. He would have shown them the stamps first, and then made up and given them that more-or-less accurate bull story about them.

"Well, and what do you do now?" Malianov asked, feeling his heart sinking somewhere again.

No one answered. Weingarten poured himself another glass, drank it, and ate the last herring roll. Gubar watched listlessly as his strange son played with the glasses, his serious, pale face intent. Then Weingarten took up the story again, without any jokes this time, as though too weary for them, barely moving his lips. How he called Gubar, and Gubar did not answer; how he called Malianov and discovered that Snegovoi did exist; how scared he was when Malianov went to let Lidochka in and didn't come back to the phone for so long; how he didn't sleep all night, pacing his room and thinking, thinking, thinking, taking bromides and thinking some more; how he called Malianov this morning and realized that they had contacted him, too, and then Gubar came over—with his own problems.

CHAPTER 6

Excerpt 13. . . . found out that Gubar was lazy and played hooky as a child and was overly concerned with sex then, too. He dropped out of school after the ninth grade, worked as an orderly, then as a driver on a fertilizer truck, then as a lab assistant in the institute, where he met Val, and now was working in a closed research institute on some gigantic, very important project, something to do with energetics. Zakhar had no special training, but was always a radio buff; electronics was in his soul and bone marrow, and he rose quickly in the institute, even though he was held back by the lack of a diploma.

He patented several inventions, and he had two or three in the works, and he definitely did not know which one was causing all these problems. But he figured that it was last year's— he had invented something connected with "the constructive use of fading." He figured, but he wasn't sure.

The most important thing in his life had always been women. They were attracted to him like flies to honey. And when for some reason they stopped sticking to him, he began sticking to them. He had been married once and retained the most unpleasant memories and bitter lessons from the union; he now maintained the strictest code in relation to that institution. In short, he was a lady-killer of the highest degree, and in comparison with him, Weingarten looked like an ascetic, anchorite, and stoic. But for all that, he was no lecher.

He treated his women with respect, even awe, and apparently saw himself as a humble source of their pleasure. He never had two lovers at the same time; he never got into fights or ugly scenes with them, and he never, apparently, hurt any of them. So in that area, from the time his unhappy marriage ended, everything was going very well. Until very recently.

He himself felt that the unpleasantness brought on by the space aliens began with the appearance of a repulsive rash on his feet. He rushed to a doctor as soon as the rash appeared, because he always took good care of his health. The doctor calmed him down, gave him some pills, and the rash went away. But then came the invasion of women. They came in droves—all the women he had ever been involved with. They hung around his apartment in twos and threes; there was one horrible day when there were five women in his apartment at the same time. And he simply did not understand what they wanted from him. And, worse than that, he had the sneaking suspicion that the women didn't know either. They abused him; they groveled at his feet; they begged for something or other; they fought among themselves like cats; they broke all his dishes, shattered the blue Japanese water bowl, and ruined his furniture. They had hysterical fits; they tried poisoning themselves, some threatened to poison him, and they were inexhaustible and extremely demanding in lovemaking. And many of them had been married a long time, loved their husbands and children, and the husbands also came to Gubar's apartment and behaved strangely. (Gubar mumbled more than ever in this part of the story.)

In brief, his life had turned into hell; he lost fifteen pounds; he had a rash all over his body; there was no question of doing his work, and he had to take an unpaid leave of absence even though he was deep in debt. (At first, he sought refuge from the onslaught at the institute, but very quickly realized that this would only lead to his personal problems hitting the public limelight. He also mumbled this part.)

This hell lasted ten days nonstop and suddenly ended the day before yesterday. He had just turned over the last of the women to her husband, a gloomy police sergeant, when a woman appeared with a child. He remembered the woman. He'd met her six years ago. They had been in a crowded bus, squeezed together. He looked at her, and he liked what he saw. Excuse me, he said, would you have a piece of paper and a pencil? Yes, here you are, she replied, taking the needed articles from her purse. Thank you so much, he said, now please write down your name and phone number. They had a wonderful time on the Riga seashore and parted quietly—it seemed never to meet again, pleased with each other and no strings attached.

And now she appeared on his doorstep with the boy and said he was his son. She had been married for three years to a very good and very famous man, whom she loved and respected deeply. She could not explain to Gubar why she had come. She cried every time he tried to find out. She wrung her hands, and it was apparent that she felt her behavior was immoral and criminal. But she would not leave. The days that she spent in Gubar's ravaged apartment were the worst part of the nightmare. She behaved like a sleepwalker, talking all the time. Gubar could understand the words, but there was no way he could make any sense of them. And then yesterday morning she woke up. She pulled Gubar out of bed, led him to the bathroom, turned on the water full blast, and whispered an absolutely unbelievable tale into Gubar's ear.

According to her (in Gubar's interpretation) it seemed that since ancient times there had been this secret, semimystical Union of the Nine on Earth. These were monstrously secretive wise men, either very long-lived or immortal, who

were concerned with only two things: first, that they gather
and master all the achievements of every single branch of science, and second, that they make sure that none of the new
scientific-technological advances be used by people for self-
destruction. These wise men are almost all-knowing and
practically all-powerful. It is impossible to hide from them,
and it is no use fighting them. And now this Union of the
Nine was taking on Zakhar Gubar. Why him—she did not
know. What Gubar was supposed to do now she didn't know
either. He had to figure that out for himself. She only knew
that all the recent unpleasantnesses he had had were a warning. And she was sent to him as a warning too. And so that
Zakhar would remember the warning, she had been ordered
to leave the boy with him. Who gave the order she didn't know.
In fact, she knew nothing else. And didn't want to know. She
only wanted to be sure that nothing bad happened to the boy.
She begged Gubar not to resist and to think twenty times before taking any action. And now she had to go.

Weeping, her face buried in her handkerchief, she left.
And Gubar was left with the boy. One on one. What took place
between them until three in the afternoon, he didn't wish to
tell. But something did happen.

(The boy had a brief statement on the matter: "I straightened him out is all.") At three p.m. Gubar couldn't stand it
anymore, and he called and then ran over to see Weingarten,
his closest friend.

"I still don't understand a thing," he concluded. "I listened
to Val and I listened to you, Dmitri. I still don't understand.
Maybe it's the heat? They say it hasn't been this hot in two
hundred and fifty years. And we've all gone mad, each in his
own way."

"Wait a minute, Zakhar," Weingarten said, frowning.
"You're a stable person, so don't start hypothesizing just yet."

"What hypothesis!" Gubar said unhappily. "It's clear to me without any hypothesis that we won't come up with anything here. We have to report this to the right place, that's what I say."

Weingarten gave him a withering look.

"And where do you propose we report this information?"

"How should I know? There has to be some organization. Some local agency."

The boy giggled loudly, and Gubar shut up. Malianov pictured Weingarten reporting in at the appropriate agency, telling the interested investigator his tall tale of the red-haired midget in the tight-fitting black suit. Gubar looked rather funny in the same situation. And as for Malianov himself . . .

"Well, fellows, you do what you like, but the police station is not the place for me. A man died under strange circumstances across the hall from me, and I am the last one to have seen him alive. And there's no point in my going anyway, I have the feeling they'll come for me."

Weingarten immediately poured him a glass of cognac, and Malianov gulped it down, without even tasting it. Weingarten said with a sigh:

"Yes, buddies. There's nobody to consult with. One word and they'll stick us in the nuthouse. We'll have to figure it out ourselves. Go on, Dmitri, go ahead. You have a clear head. Go on, figure it out."

Malianov rubbed his forehead.

"Actually, my head is stuffed," he said. "I have nothing to say. It's all a nightmare. I do understand one thing: You were told straight out to drop your work. I was told nothing, but my life was made into—"

"Right!" Weingarten interrupted. "Fact number one: Someone does not like our work. Question: Who? Be observant: An alien comes to see me." Weingarten ticked the points off on his fingers. "An agent from the Union of the Nine to see Zakhar. By the way, have you heard of the Union of the Nine? I have the name in the back of my head, I must have read about it or something, but I don't remember where. Nobody comes to see you. That is, of course you are visited, but by agents in disguise. What is the conclusion to be drawn here?"

"Well?" Malianov asked gloomily.

"The conclusion that follows is that there are no aliens and no ancient wise men, but something else, some force—and our work is getting in its way."

"That's nonsense," Malianov said. "Delirium. Just crap. Think a bit. I'm working on stars in the gas-dust cloud. You have that revertase. And Zakhar is really out in left field— applied electronics." He suddenly remembered. "Snegovoi had talked about that, too. You know what he said? He said, there's the estate, and there's the water. I only just now figured out what he meant by that. The poor guy was busting his brains over it, too. Or maybe you think there are three different pow- ers at work here?" he asked acidly.

"No, buddy, now just hold on!" Weingarten insisted. "Don't be in such a hurry."

He looked as though he had figured it all out long ago and would clear everything up completely if, of course, they only stopped interrupting and let him get on with it. But he didn't clear anything up—he stopped talking and stared at the empty herring jar.

They all sat in silence. Then Gubar spoke softly.

"I keep thinking about Snegovoi. I mean ... he probably was ordered to stop his work too ... and how could he? He was a military man ... His work was—"

"I have to pee!" the boy announced, and when Gubar sighed and led him off to the toilet, he added in a loud voice: "and go poo."

"No, buddy, don't you rush," Weingarten spoke again. "Just imagine for a second that there is a group of creatures on Earth powerful enough to pull off all these stunts. Let's say it's that Union of the Nine. What's important to them? To put an end to certain work in a certain field that leads to a certain goal. How do you know? Maybe there are another hundred people in Leningrad going crazy like us. And maybe a hundred thousand all over the world. And like us, they're afraid to admit it. Some are afraid and some are embarrassed. And maybe some are happy! They're making attractive offers, you know."

"I haven't gotten any attractive offers," Malianov said gloomily.

"And that's by design too! You're a jerk, with no interest in money. You don't even know how to bribe the right person at the right time. The whole world is one big obstacle to you. All the tables are reserved at a restaurant, that's an obstacle. There's a line for tickets, and that's an obstacle. Somebody's making time with your woman, and—"

"All right! That's enough! I don't need a lecture."

"No. Just knock it off, buddy. It's a completely possible supposition. It means, of course, that they're mighty powerful, fantastically so ... but, damn it all, hypnosis and suggestion do exist, and maybe even, damn it, telepathic suggestion! No, buddy, just imagine: There is a race, an ancient race, wise, and maybe not even human—our competition. They've been waiting patiently, gathering data, preparing. And now they've decided to deliver the *coup de grace*. Note, not by open warfare, but much more cleverly. They realize that creating mountains of bodies is pointless, barbaric, and dangerous for them as well. And so they decide to operate carefully, with a scalpel, along the central nervous system, the foundation of all foundations, the most promising research. Get it?"

Malianov heard him and didn't hear him. A disgusting

feeling was climbing up to his throat. He wanted to shut his ears, go away, lie down, stretch out, hide his head under a pillow. It was fear. And not plain ordinary fear, but the Black Fear. Get away from here. Run for your life. Drop everything, hide, bury yourself, drown. Hey you, he shouted at himself. Wake up, you idiot! You can't do that, you'll die. And he spoke with effort.

"I get it, but it's nonsense."

"Why?"

"Because that's a fairy tale." His voice got hoarse and he coughed. "For young readers. Why don't you write it down and take it over to Campfire Publications. Make sure Pioneer Vasya breaks up the evil gang in the end and saves the world."

"All right," Weingarten said very calmly. "These events did happen to us?"

"Well, yes."

"The events were fantastic?"

"Well, let's say that they were."

"Well then, buddy, how do you expect to explain fantastic events without a fantastic hypothesis?"

"I don't know anything about it," Malianov said. "You two have fantastic events. And maybe you've both been drinking like crazy for the last two weeks. Nothing fantastic has happened to me. I'm not a heavy drinker."

Weingarten's face turned beet red and he slammed his fist on the table and shouted, "Goddamn it, you have to believe us, if we don't believe each other, goddamn it, then everything would just go to hell! Maybe that was what those bastards were counting on, goddamn it! That we wouldn't believe each other, that we would all end up alone, each to be manipulated as they want."

He was shouting and sputtering so wildly that Malianov got scared. He even forgot about the Black Fear. "Well, all right," he said, "come on, knock it off, don't get hysterical. It was just a mistake on my part, I'm sorry. I'm sorry, I didn't mean it." Gubar came back from the toilet and stared at them, terrified.

Through with his shouting, Weingarten leaped up, grabbed a bottle of mineral water from the refrigerator, tore off the plastic cap with his teeth, and drank from the bottle. The carbonated water poured down his stubbly fat cheeks and immediately appeared in the form of sweat on his forehead and bare, hairy shoulders.

"I mean, what I really had in mind," Malianov said placatingly, "is that I don't like it when impossible things are explained away by impossible causes. You know, Occam's razor. Otherwise you come up with God knows what."

"So, what's your suggestion?" said Weingarten, placated, stuffing the empty bottle under the table.

"I don't have one. If I did, I'd tell you. My brain's been numbed by fear. Only it seems to me that if they're really so all-powerful, they could have managed the whole thing a lot more simply."

"How, for instance?"

"Oh, I don't know. Well, they could have poisoned you with rotten canned goods. And Zakhar—given him a thousand-volt shock. And anyway, why even bother with all this killing and terror? If they're such hotshot telepathists, they could have made us forget everything beyond simple math. Or created a conditioned reflex: as soon as we sat down to work, we'd get the runs, or the flu: drippy nose, achy head. Or eczema. There's lots of stuff. Quietly, peacefully, no one would have even noticed."

Weingarten was just waiting for him to finish.

"Look, Dmitri, you have to understand one thing."

But Zakhar did not let him finish.

"Just a minute!" he pleaded, putting out his hands as though to lead Weingarten and Malianov to their separate corners. "Let me talk, while I still remember. Will you wait, Val, and let me talk? It's about headaches. You just mentioned them, Dmitri. You know, I was hospitalized last year."

It turned out that he was in the hospital the year before because there was something wrong with his blood, and he shared a room with this Vladlen Semenovich Glukhov, an orientalist. Glukhov was there with a heart condition, but that wasn't the point. The point was that they got to be friends and met once in a while after they got out. And, just two months ago, that same Glukhov complained to Gubar that he had this huge project for which he had been gathering material for ten years and it was all going to hell because of a strange idiosyncrasy that Glukhov had developed. Namely: As soon as he sat down to write up his research, his head began aching terribly, to the point of nausea and fainting spells.

"And yet he would think about his work freely," Zakhar continued, "read materials, and even, I think, talk about it ... though I'm not sure, and I don't want to lie to you. But he couldn't write about it at all. And after what you just said, Dmitri ..."

"Do you know his address?" Weingarten demanded.

"Yes."

"Does he have a phone?"

"Yes. I have the number."

"Go ahead, invite him over here. He's one of us."

Malianov jumped up.

"Go to hell!" he shouted. "You're nuts! You can't do that. Maybe he's just got a thing about it."

"We all have a thing."

"Val, he's an orientalist! A completely different field!"

"It's the same one, buddy, I swear it's the same one."

"Don't do it! Zakhar, sit down, don't listen to him. He's drunker than a coot."

It was horrible and impossible to picture a normal and total stranger coming into this hot, smoke-filled kitchen and immersing himself in the pervasive madness, terror, and drunkenness.

"Look, why don't we do this?" Malianov insisted. "Why don't we call Vecherovsky? I swear it'll do more good."

Weingarten had no objections to Vecherovsky. "Right," he said. "That's a good idea, calling Vecherovsky. Vecherovsky, he's got a head on his shoulders. Zakhar, go call your Glukhov, and then we'll call Vecherovsky."

Malianov desperately didn't want any Glukhovs. He begged, he pleaded, he insisted that it was his house and that he was going to throw all of them out on their ears. But it was no good going against Weingarten. Zakhar went off to call Glukhov, and the boy slipped off the stool and followed him like a shadow.

CHAPTER 7

Excerpt 14.... Zakhar's son, comfortably ensconced on the corner of the bed, graced the proceedings with occasional readings from the *Popular Medical Encyclopedia*, given to him by Malianov to keep him quiet. Vecherovsky, strikingly elegant in contrast to the sweaty, disheveled Weingarten, listened and looked at the strange boy curiously, raising his red eyebrows high. He had not yet said anything substantial—he had asked a few questions that had, to Malianov (and not to Malianov alone), seemed irrelevant. For instance, for no reason at all, he asked Zakhar if he was often in conflict with his supervisors and Glukhov if he liked to watch television. (It turned out that Zakhar never had conflicts with anybody, that was his personality, and Glukhov did like to watch television, not only liked it, but couldn't resist it.)

Malianov really liked Glukhov. In general, Malianov didn't like seeing new people in old company; he was always afraid they would misbehave somehow and he would be embarrassed for them. But Glukhov turned out to be okay. He was extremely cozy and unthreatening—a little scrawny, snub-nosed fellow with reddish eyes hidden by strong glasses. When he arrived he happily drank the glass of vodka Weingarten offered him and was visibly saddened when he learned it was the last one in the house. When he was subjected to cross-examination, he listened to each one attentively, leaning his head professorially to the right and looking to the right as well. "No, no," he replied apologetically. "No, nothing like that happened to me. Please, I can't even imagine anything like that. My thesis? I'm afraid it's too foreign for you: 'The Cultural Influence of the USA on Japan: An Attempt at a Qualitative and Quantitative Analysis.' Yes, my headaches seem to be some idiosyncrasy: I've discussed it with major doctors—a rare case, they said."

In general, they laid an egg with Glukhov, but it didn't matter, it was nice that he was there. He was a real down-to-earth guy. He drank heartily and wanted more, ate caviar with childlike glee, preferred Ceylon tea, and his favorite reading matter was mysteries. He watched the strange child with reserved apprehension, laughing uncertainly from time to time, listened to the delirious tales with uncommon sympathy, and scratched behind both ears, muttering, "Yes, that's amazing, unbelievable!" In a word, everything about Glukhov was clear to Malianov. There would be no new information and certainly no advice coming from him.

Weingarten, as usual when Vecherovsky was around, lowered his profile. He even looked more presentable and stopped shouting and calling people "buddy." However, he did eat the last grains of the black caviar.

If you didn't count the brief replies to Vecherovsky's questions, Zakhar said nothing. He didn't even get to tell his own story—Weingarten took that upon himself. And he stopped admonishing his son and just smiled painfully as he listened to the helpful quotations about the diseases of various delicate organs.

And so they sat in silence. Sipping cold tea. Smoking. The windows of the house across the street shone molten gold, the silver sickle of the new moon hung in the dark blue sky, and there was a sharp crackling sound coming through the window—they must have been burning old crates again on the street. Weingarten rustled his pack of cigarettes, peeked inside, crumpled it up, and softly asked: "Who's got any cigarettes left?" "Here, help yourself," Zakhar replied in a low voice. Glukhov coughed and rattled his teaspoon in the glass.

Malianov looked over at Vecherovsky. He was sitting in his chair, his legs stretched out and crossed at the ankles, studying the nails of his right hand. Malianov looked at Weingarten. Weingarten was smoking and watching Vecherovsky over the glowing tip of his cigarette. Zakhar was looking at Vecherovsky. And Glukhov. Malianov was struck by the silliness of the situation. What, actually, do we expect from him? So, he's a mathematician. So, a major mathematician. So, let's say he's a very major mathematician—a world-famous mathematician. So? We're like a bunch of children. God! We're lost in the woods and trustingly flutter our eyes at the nice man: Oh, he'll lead us out.

"Well, basically, that's all the ideas we have on the matter," Weingarten said smoothly. "As you can see, there are at least two positions shaping up." He spoke as though addressing the group, but looked only at Vecherovsky. "Dmitri feels that we should try to explain all these events in the framework of known natural phenomena. I feel that we are dealing with the intervention of forces completely unknown to us. That is: like cures like, fantastic with the fantastic."

That tirade sounded unbelievably phony. No, he couldn't just simply say, we're lost, mister, lead us out; no, he had to sum things up: We've been doing some thinking too. And now sit there like a fool. Malianov picked up the teapot and left Val to his shame. He did not hear the conversation while he ran the water and put on the kettle. When he returned, Vecherovsky was speaking slowly, carefully examining the nails on his left hand.

"... and that's why I feel your point of view is more accurate. Really, the fantastic should be explained by the fantastic. I suspect that all of you have fallen into the sphere of interest of ... let's call it a supercivilization. I think that's become the standard term for an intelligence many degrees more powerful than human intelligence."

Weingarten inhaled deeply and, exhaling smoke, nodded with an important and concentrated air.

"Why they need to stop your research in particular," continued Vecherovsky, "is not only a complex question, but an academic one. The point is that humanity, without even suspecting it, has attracted the attention of this intelligence and stopped being a self-contained system. Apparently, without even suspecting it, we've trod on the corns of some supercivilization, and that supercivilization, apparently, has decided to regulate our progress as it sees fit."

"Phil," Malianov said. "Wait. Don't you see it either? What the hell kind of supercivilization is this? Some supercivilization that prods us like a blind kitten. Why all this meaningless nonsense? My investigator and the cognac? Zakhar's women? Where is the fundamental principle of reason: expediency, economy?"

"Those are particulars," Vecherovsky replied softly. "Why measure nonhuman expediency in human terms? And then remember with what force you smack yourself on the cheek to kill a crummy mosquito. A blow like that could easily kill all the mosquitoes in the vicinity."

Weingarten added: "Or, for instance. What is the expediency of building a bridge over a river from the point of view of a trout?"

"Well, I don't know," Malianov said. "It just doesn't make sense."

Vecherovsky waited a while and then, certain that Malianov had stopped talking, continued.

"I would like to stress the following. When the question is put this way, your personal problems recede into the
background. We're talking about the fate of mankind. Well,
perhaps not in the fatal sense of the word, but the fate of its
dignity in any case. So now our goal is to protect not only your
revertase, Val, but the future of our whole planet's biology. Or
am I wrong?"

For the first time in Vecherovsky's presence Val blew up to
his usual proportions. He nodded most energetically but said
something that Malianov did not expect at all.

He said: "Yes, absolutely. We all understand that we're not
talking just about us here. We're talking about hundreds of research projects. Maybe thousands. What am I saying—about
the future of research in general!"

"So," Vecherovsky said energetically, "there is a battle ahead
of us. Their weapon is secrecy, therefore ours will be publicity.
The first thing we should do is tell all our friends who, on the
one hand, have enough imagination to believe us and, on the
other, enough authority to convince their colleagues who hold
high posts in science. In that way we will enter into contact
with the government obliquely and gain access to the mass
media. We will then be able to inform all mankind if necessary. Your first move was absolutely correct. You turned to me.
I will personally attempt to convince several major mathematicians who are at the same time important administrators. I
will begin, naturally, with our own people, and then move on
to foreign mathematicians."

He was animated, sitting up straight, and talking and talking and talking. He mentioned names, titles, positions; he
clearly defined who Malianov should see and who Weingarten

should turn to. You would have thought that he had been planning this for days. But the more he talked, the more depressed Malianov became. And when Vecherovsky, with totally indecent agitation, moved on to part two of his program, the apotheosis—when humanity, united by the general alarm, fights off the supercivilized enemy shoulder to shoulder across the entire planet—well, then Malianov felt that he'd had it, stood up, and went into the kitchen to make fresh tea. So much for Vecherovsky. Some brain. The poor guy must have been terrified too. This is no simple argument about telepathy. But it's our own fault: Vecherovsky this, Vecherovsky that. Vecherovsky is just an ordinary man. A smart man, yes, a major figure, but no more than that. As long as you talk about abstractions, he's terrific, but when it's real life ... That Vecherovsky immediately took Val's side and didn't even want to hear him out really hurt. Malianov took the teapot and went back into the room.

Naturally, Weingarten was letting Vecherovsky have it: Deep respect is deep respect, but when a man is blathering nonsense, no amount of respect is going to help. Maybe Vecherovsky thinks he's dealing with total idiots. Maybe Vecherovsky has a couple of authoritative and feeble-minded academicians stowed away somewhere who will greet this news with great enthusiasm after a bottle or two. He, Weingarten, did not personally have any academicians like that. He, Weingarten, had his old friend Dmitri Malianov, from whom he expected some definite sympathy, especially since Malianov was in the same pickle. And what happened—did he welcome his tale of woe with enthusiasm? With interest? With at least sympathy? The hell he did! The first thing he said was that Weingarten was a liar—and in his own way, Malianov is right. Weingarten is terrified to even think about approaching his boss with a story like that even though his boss is still a young man, not yet ossified, and well disposed to a certain noble madness in science. He doesn't know Vecherovsky's situation, but he, Weingarten, has no intention of spending the rest of his days in even the most luxurious of nuthouses.

"The orderlies will come and take us away!" Zakhar said woefully. "That's clear. It's okay for you guys, but they'll brand me a sex maniac as well."

"Hold on, Zakhar," Weingarten said in irritation. "No, Phil, I just don't recognize you! Let's assume that all our talk of mental institutions is an exaggeration. This will still mean the end of our careers as scientists, immediately! Our reputations will be ruined! And then, goddamn it, even if we did find one or two sympathetic souls in the Academy, how can they go to the government with this ranting? Who would want to risk doing that? You know what kind of pressure would have to be brought on a man for him to risk that? And for humanity, our dear co-inhabitants of planet Earth . . ." Weingarten waved his hand and looked at Malianov with his olive eyes. "Pour me some hot tea," he said. "Publicity . . . publicity is a two-ended stick, you know." And he began slurping his tea, rubbing the back of his hairy arm across his nose.

"Who would like some more?" Malianov asked.

He tried not to look at Vecherovsky. He poured some for Zakhar, for Glukhov. For himself. He sat down. He was terribly sorry for Vecherovsky and very uncomfortable for him. Val was right: A scientist's reputation is a fragile thing. One unsuccessful speech, and then where is your reputation, Philip Pavlovich Vecherovsky?

Vecherovsky was huddled up in the chair, his face in his hands. It was unbearable.

"You see, Phil, all your suggestions, your plan of action, it's probably all correct in theory," Malianov said. "But we don't need theory now. We need a plan that can be realized in real circumstances. You say: a united mankind. You see, for your plan, there may be some life-form that could do it, but not ours, not earthlings, I mean. Our people would never believe anything like that. You know when it will believe in a supercivilization? When that supercivilization stoops to our level and starts sprinkling us with bombs from whining spacecraft. Then we'll believe, then we'll be united, and even then not right away. We'll probably wallop each other with a few salvos first."

"That's it exactly!" Weingarten agreed in an unpleasant voice and laughed curtly.

No one said anything.

"And my boss is a woman, anyway," Zakhar said. "Very nice, very sweet, but how can I tell her about all this? About me, I mean?"

They all sat there silently sipping tea. Then Glukhov spoke softly.

"What wonderful tea! You really are a specialist, Dmitri. I haven't had tea like this in ages. Yes ... of course, all this is difficult and unclear. On the other hand, look at the sky, what a beautiful moon. Tea, a smoke—what else does man need? A good detective series on television? I don't know. Now, you, Dmitri, you're doing something with stars, with interstellar gases. Really, what business is it of yours? Just think about it. Something doesn't want you to pry. Well, the answer is simple: Just don't. Drink tea, watch television. The heavens aren't for spying on—they're for admiring."

And then Zakhar's boy announced out loud:

"You're a sneak!"

Malianov thought that he meant Glukhov. But no. The boy, squinting like an adult, was looking at Vecherovsky and threatening him with a chocolate-covered finger.

"Sh, sh," Zakhar whispered helplessly. Vecherovsky

suddenly took his hands from his face and resumed his original position—lounging in the chair with his legs stretched out
and crossed at the ankles. There was a grin on his face.

"So," he said, "I am happy to prove that Comrade Weingarten's hypothesis leads us to a dead end that is obvious to
the naked eye. It's easy to see that the hypothesis about the
legendary Union of the Nine will lead us to the same dead end,
as will the mysterious intelligence hiding in the depths of the
seas or any other rational force. It would be very good if you
all stopped and thought for a minute to convince yourselves of
the correctness of what I say."

Malianov stirred his tea and thought: The bastard! Did
he have us going! Why? What's the play-acting for? Weingarten was staring straight ahead, his eyes bulging slowly, his fat,
sweaty cheeks twitching threateningly. Glukhov was staring at
everyone in turn, and Zakhar waited patiently—the drama of
the minute's pause completely escaping him.

Then Vecherovsky spoke again.

"Note. In order to explain fantastic events we tried to use
concepts that, however fantastic, still belonged in the realm
of contemporary understanding. That yielded nothing. Absolutely nothing. Val proved that to us quite convincingly.
Therefore, obviously, there is no point in applying concepts
from outside the realm of contemporary understanding. Say,
for instance, God or ... or something else. Conclusion?"

Weingarten wiped his face nervously with his shirt and
attacked his tea feverishly. Malianov asked in an injured tone:

"You mean, you were just making fools of us on purpose?"

"What else could I do?" Vecherovsky replied, raising his
damn red eyebrows to the ceiling. "Prove to you that going
to the authorities was useless? That it was meaningless to put
the question the way you were? The Union of the Nine or Fu
Manchu—what's the difference? What is there to argue about?

Whatever answer you got, there could be no practical course of action based on it. When your house burns down or is destroyed by a hurricane or is carried away by flood—you don't think about what precisely happened to the house, you think about how you're going to live, where you're going to live, and what to do next."

"You're trying to say . . ." began Malianov.

"I'm saying that nothing *interesting* happened to you. There is nothing to be interested in here, nothing to study, nothing to analyze. All your seeking of causes is nothing more than wasteful idle curiosity. You shouldn't be thinking about what kind of press is squeezing you; you should be thinking about how to behave under the pressure. And thinking about that is much more complex than fantasizing about King Asoka, because from now on each of you is *alone*! No one will help you. No one will give you any advice. No one will decide for you. Not the academicians, not the government, not even progressive humanity—Val made that perfectly clear for you."

He stood, poured himself some tea, and returned to his chair—intolerably confident, pulled together, elegantly casual, still looking like a peer at a diplomatic reception at the palace.

The boy read aloud:

"'If the patient does not follow doctor's orders, does not take his medication, and abuses alcohol, then approximately five or six years later the secondary phase is followed by the disease's third—and last—stage.'"

Zakhar sighed.

"But why? Why me?"

Vecherovsky placed the cup in the saucer with a light clatter and put the saucer on the table next to him.

"Because our age is wearing black," he explained, dabbing his pinkish gray equine lips with a snowy white handkerchief.

"It is still wearing a tall top hat, and still we continue to run, and when the clock strikes the hour of inaction and the hour of leave-taking from daily cares, then comes the moment of division, and we no longer dream of anything—"

"The hell with you," Malianov said, and Vecherovsky pealed with smug Martian guffaws.

Weingarten fished a longish butt out of the ashtray, stuck it between his fat lips, struck a match, and sat for a while, his crossed eyes focused on the glowing tip.

"Really," he muttered, "does it really matter what power ... as long as it is more powerful than humans?" He inhaled. "An aphid squashed by a brick and an aphid squashed by a coin ... but I'm no aphid. I can choose."

Zakhar looked at him hopefully, but Weingarten said nothing else. Choose, thought Malianov. That's easy enough to say.

"That's easy enough to say—choose!" Zakhar began, but Glukhov started talking. Zakhar looked at him hopefully.

"But it's clear," Glukhov said with unusual feeling. "Isn't it obvious which you should choose? You must choose life! What else? Surely not your telescopes and test tubes. Let them choke on your telescopes! And interstellar gases! You have to live, love, feel nature—really *feel* it, not dig around in it! When I look at a tree or a bush now, I feel, I know that it is my friend, that we exist for each other, that we need each other."

"Now?" Vecherovsky asked loudly.

Glukhov stuttered to a stop.

"Excuse me?"

"We've met, you know, Vladlen," Vecherovsky said. "Remember? Estonia, the math-linguistics school? The sauna, the beer."

"Yes, yes," Glukhov said, lowering his eyes. "Yes."

"You were quite different then," Vecherovsky said.

"Well, back then ..." Glukhov began. "Barons grow old, you know."

"Barons also struggle," Vecherovsky said. "It wasn't so long ago."

Glukhov spread his hands in silence.

Malianov understood nothing of this interlude, but there was something to it, something unpleasant, sinister, there was some reason for what they were saying to each other. And Zakhar, apparently, had understood, in his own way. Malianov felt some insult to himself in that brief exchange, because suddenly, with unusual harshness, almost with anger, he shouted at Vecherovsky:

"They killed Snegovoi! It's easy for you to talk, Philip, they don't have you by the throat, you're all right!"

Vecherovsky nodded.

"Yes," he said. "I'm all right. I'm all right, and Vladlen here is all right, too. Right, Vladlen?"

The little cozy man with the bunny-rabbit eyes behind the strong glasses in steel frames spread his hands again in silence. Then he stood up and, avoiding everyone's eyes, said:

"Excuse me, friends, but it's time for me to go. It's getting late."

CHAPTER 8

Excerpt 15. . . . Do you want to spend the night at my place?"
Vecherovsky asked.

Malianov was washing the dishes and thinking over the of-
fer. Vecherovsky wasn't rushing him for a reply. He went back
into the room, moved around in there for a while, and then returned with a mound of garbage in a soggy newspaper, which
he threw into the garbage can. Then he picked up a towel and
wiped off the kitchen table.

Actually, after all of the day's events and conversations,
Malianov didn't feel like being alone. On the other hand, it
wasn't very nice to abandon the apartment and run off; it was
almost shameful. It'll look like they managed to run me out
after all, he thought. And I hate sleeping over, even at friends'
houses. Even at Vecherovsky's. He suddenly smelled the
aroma of coffee. That pink cup, as delicate as a rose petal, and
in it—the magical elixir *à la* Vecherovsky. But when you think
about it, you don't drink that at bedtime. He could have coffee
in the morning.

He washed the last saucer, put it into the drainer, wiped
up the puddle on the linoleum haphazardly, and went into
his room. Vecherovsky was in the armchair, facing the window. The sky was golden pink and the new moon was perched
just above the high-rise building, like on a minaret. Malianov turned his chair to the window and sat down. They

were separated by the desk, which Vecherovsky had cleared up: the notebooks were in an orderly pile, there wasn't even a trace of the week's supply of dust, and the three pencils and the pen were neatly lined up by the calendar. While Malianov had done the dishes, Vecherovsky managed to make the room sparkle—all it lacked was a vacuuming—yet he remained elegant, suave, and without a single spot on his creamy suit. He didn't even get sweaty, which was absolutely fantastic. While Malianov, even though he had worn Irina's apron, had a wet belly, like Weingarten's. If a woman's belly is wet after doing the dishes, it means her husband is a drunkard. But what if the husband's belly is wet?

They sat in silence, watching the lights go out one by one in the twelve-story building. Kaliam showed up, mewing softly; he hopped up into Vecherovsky's lap and began purring. Vecherovsky petted him with his long, narrow hand without taking his eyes off the lights in the window.

"He sheds," Malianov warned.

"No matter," Vecherovsky replied softly.

They fell silent once again. Now, when there was no sweaty Weingarten or terrified Zakhar with that abominable child of his or that ordinary yet mysterious Glukhov, when there was only Vecherovsky, infinitely calm and infinitely self-confident and not expecting any supernatural decisions from anyone— now it all seemed like a dream, or even some bizarre fairy tale. If it had actually happened, well, it was long ago, and it didn't actually happen, it stopped just before it started. Malianov even sensed a vague interest in that semifictional hero: Did he get sentenced to fifteen years or was it all ...

Excerpt 16. ... remembered Snegovoi and the gun in his pajamas and the seal on the door.

"Listen," I said, "did they really kill Snegovoi?"

"Who?" Vecherovsky answered after a pause.

"Well, uh," I began and stopped.

"Snegovoi, judging by everything, shot himself," Vecherovsky said. "He couldn't stand it."

"Couldn't stand what?"

"The pressure. He made his choice."

Now it wasn't a bizarre fairy tale. I felt that familiar fear inside and I tucked my feet under me on the chair and hugged my knees. I curled up so tight my muscles crackled. It was me and it was happening to me. Not to Ivan the Tsarevich, not to Ivan the Wise Fool—not to any fairy-tale hero—but to me. Vecherovsky could talk, he was safe.

"Listen," I said through clenched teeth. "What's with you and Glukhov? That was a strange conversation you two had."

"He made me angry."

"How?"

Vecherovsky didn't answer right away.

"He doesn't dare be alone," he said.

"I don't understand," I said after some thought.

"What gets me is not how he made his choice," Vecherovsky said slowly, as though thinking aloud. "But why keep justifying his action? And not simply justifying it, but trying to convince others to follow him. He's ashamed to be weak among strong people, and he wants you to be weak too. He thinks that it will be easier for him. Maybe he's even right, but that attitude of his infuriates me."

I listened to him, mouth wide open, and when he was through, I asked:

"Do you mean that Glukhov is also . . . under pressure?"

"He *was* under pressure. He's simply squashed now."

"Wait a minute."

Vecherovsky turned his face to me slowly:

"You didn't understand?"

"What do you mean? He said . . . I heard him with my own ears . . . I mean, you can see, simply, that he hadn't dreamed or imagined . . . it's obvious!"

But it didn't seem so obvious to me anymore. On the contrary.

"Then you didn't understand," Vecherovsky said, looking at me with curiosity. "Zakhar did." He got his pipe for the first time that evening and calmly started filling it. "Strange that you didn't understand. Well, you were obviously upset. Judge for yourself: The man loves mysteries, loves watching television, his favorite show is on today, but for some reason he rushed over to visit with total strangers—for what? To complain about his headaches?" He struck a match and lit his pipe. An orange flame danced in his eyes. He sucked on the pipe. "And then, I recognized him right away. Actually, not right away. He's changed considerably. He was a live wire— energetic, excitable, sarcastic. None of this Rousseauism and no vodka drinking. First I just felt sorry for him, but when he started singing the praises of his new philosophy, I got mad."

He concentrated on his pipe.

I rolled up into a tighter ball. So that's how it was. The man had been squashed. He was still alive but no longer the same man. Broken flesh, broken spirit. What did they do to him that he couldn't take it? But there must be pressures, I guess, that no man can take.

"So, you mean you condemn Snegovoi, too?" I asked.

"I don't condemn anyone," Vecherovsky countered.

"Well . . . you're incensed by Glukhov."

"You didn't understand," Vecherovsky said with some impatience. "I'm not incensed by Glukhov's choice. What right have I to be incensed by a choice made by a man left one on one, without help, without hope. I'm annoyed by Glukhov's behavior after his decision. I repeat: He's ashamed of his

choice and that's why—and only because of that—he's trying
to convert others to his faith. In other words, because of his
self-image he's adding to the already unbearable pressure he
feels. Understand?"

"With my mind, yes."

I wanted to add that Glukhov was completely understandable and if he could be understood, he could be forgiven,
that Glukhov was beyond the realm of analysis, in a realm
where only compassion was applicable, but I realized that
I didn't have the strength to talk. I was shivering. Without
help and without hope. Without help and without hope. Why
me? What for? What did I do to them? I had to hold up my
end of the conversation, and I said, clenching my teeth after
every word:

"After all, there are pressures that no man in the world
could bear."

Vecherovsky answered something, but I didn't hear him
or I didn't understand it. I was realizing that just yesterday I
was a man, a member of society. I had my own concerns and
worries, yes, but as long as I obeyed the laws created by the
system—and that had become a habit—as long as I obeyed
those laws, I was protected from all imaginable dangers by the
police, the army, the unions, public opinion, and my friends
and family. Now, something in the world around me had gone
haywire. Suddenly I became a catfish holed up in a crack, sur-
rounded by monstrous vague shadows that didn't even need
huge looming jaws—a slight movement of their fins would
grind me into a powder, squash me, turn me into zilch. And
it was made clear to me that as long as I hid in that crack I
would not be touched. Yet it was even more terrifying than
that. I was separated from humanity the way a lamb is cut
off from the herd and dragged off somewhere for some unknown reason, while the herd, unsuspecting, goes on about its

business, moving farther away into the distance. I would have felt much better if only they had been warlike aliens, some bloodthirsty, destructive aggressors from outer space, from the ocean depths, from the fourth dimension. I would have been one among many; there would have been a place for me, work for me; I would be in the ranks! But I was doomed to perish in front of everyone's eyes. No one would see a thing, and when I was destroyed, ground to dust, everyone would be surprised and then shrug it off. Thank God Irina wasn't around. Thank God this wasn't affecting her! A nightmare! Unbelievable nonsense! I shook my head as hard as I could. This whole mess because I'm working on interstellar matter?

"Apparently, yes," Vecherovsky said.

I stared at him in horror.

"Listen, Phil, it doesn't make any sense!" I said desperately.

"From the human point of view, none at all," Vecherovsky said. "But it's not *people* who have something against your work."

"Then who does?"

"There you go again—a question as good as gold," Vecherovsky said, and it was so unlike him that I laughed. Nervously. Hysterically. And I heard his satisfied Martian guffaws.

"Listen," I said, "the hell with them all. Let's have some tea."

I was afraid that Vecherovsky would say that it was time for him to go, that he had to give exams tomorrow or finish his chapter, so I hurriedly added:

"All right? I've got a box of candy hidden away—I figured, why feed Weingarten's fat face with everything. Let's indulge!"

"With pleasure," Vecherovsky said, and he got up readily.

"You know, you think and think," I said as we went into the kitchen and I put on the water. "You think and think until it all goes black. That's wrong. That's what did in Snegovoi. I know that now. He was sitting in his apartment all alone, turning on all his lights, but what good did it do? You can't light that kind of darkness with all the lamps in the world. He thought and thought and then something clicked and that was the end. You can't lose your sense of humor, that's the ticket. It really is funny, you know: All that power, all that energy—just to stop man from finding out what happens when a star falls into a dust cloud. I mean, just think about it, Phil! That's funny, isn't it?"

Vecherovsky was looking at me with an unusual expression.

"You know, Dmitri," he said, "I somehow never considered the humorous aspect of the situation."

"No? Really, when you think about it . . . So there they are and they start figuring things out: a hundred megawatts on research of annelid worms, seventy-five gigawatts for pushing through this project, and ten will be enough to stop Malianov. And someone objects that ten isn't enough. After all, you have to drive him crazy with phone calls, one; give him cognac and a woman, that's two." I sat down with my hands tight between my knees. "No, it really is funny."

"Yes," Vecherovsky agreed. "It is rather funny, but not very. Your paucity of imagination is staggering. I'm surprised you managed to come up with your bubbles."

"What bubbles!? There weren't any bubbles. And there won't be. Stop badgering me, mister director, sir. I saw nothing, heard nothing, I see no evil, hear no evil. I have a witness, I wasn't there. And anyway, my official work is on the IK spectrometer. All the rest is just the hubris of intellectuals, a Galileo complex."

We sat in silence. The teapot started to wheeze softly and make a "pf-pf-pf" noise as it got ready to boil.

"Well, all right," I said. "Paucity of imagination. Agreed. But you must admit that if you forget the fiendish details, the whole thing is fascinating. It looks like they really do exist. People gabbed so much, guessed so much, lied so much, inventing those idiotic saucers, mysterious explanations for the Baalbek terrace . . . and they really do exist. But, of course, not at all the way we had thought. I was always sure, by the way, that when they announced themselves, they would be completely different from everything we had invented about them."

"Who are 'they'?" Vecherovsky asked distractedly. He was lighting up his pipe.

"The aliens," I said. "Or to use the scientific term, the supercivilization."

"Aha," Vecherovsky said. "I get it. Nobody's ever suggested that they might be like policemen with aberrant behavior patterns."

"All right, all right," I said. I got up and set out two tea settings. "I may have a paucity of imagination, but you have none at all."

"Probably," Vecherovsky agreed. "I am totally incapable of imagining something that I think cannot exist. Phlogiston, for instance, a thermogen, or, say, the universal ether. No, no, please brew some fresh tea. And don't skimp."

"I know how to make it," I grumbled. "What were you saying about phlogiston?"

"I never believed in phlogiston. And I never believed in supercivilizations. Both phlogiston and supercivilizations are too human. Like in Baudelaire. Too human, therefore animal. Not a product of reason, a product of nonreason."

"Just a minute!" I said, with the teapot in one hand and a box of Ceylon tea in the other. "But you yourself admitted that we're dealing with a supercivilization."

"Not at all," Vecherovsky replied unflappably. "You were the ones who admitted that. I merely took advantage of the circumstances to set you straight."

The phone rang in my room. I shuddered, dropping the cover of the teapot.

"Damn," I muttered, looking back and forth between Vecherovsky and the door.

"Go on," Vecherovsky said calmly. "I'll make the tea."

I didn't pick up the phone right away. I was frightened. There was nobody who would be calling, especially at this hour. Maybe it was a drunken Weingarten? He was all alone. I picked up the phone.

"Hello?"

Weingarten's drunken voice said: "Well, of course he's not asleep. Greetings, victim of the supercivilization! How are you doing there?"

"Okay," I said with great relief. "And you?"

"Everything is shipshape," Weingarten announced. "We dropped by the Astoria. The Austeria, get it? We got a half-liter bottle, but it didn't seem like enough. So we got another one. And we took the two half-liters, that is a liter, home, and now we feel just dandy. Want to come over?"

"No," I said. "Vecherovsky is still here. We're drinking tea."

"Tea will get you teed off." Weingarten laughed. "Okay. Call if there's anything."

"I don't understand, are you alone or with Zakhar?"

"There's the three of us," Weingarten said. "It's very nice. So, if there's anything, come on over. We're waiting for you." And he hung up.

I went back to the kitchen. Vecherovsky was pouring the tea.

"Weingarten?" he asked.

"Yes, it's nice that some things are the same even in all this madness. The constancy of madness. I never used to think that a drunken Weingarten was such a good thing."

"What did he say?"

"He said 'tea will get you teed off.'"

Vecherovsky chuckled. He liked Weingarten. Very much in his own way, but he did like him. He considered Weingarten an *enfant terrible*—a big, sweaty, noisy *enfant terrible*.

I rummaged around the refrigerator and came out with an expensive box of Queen of Spades chocolates.

"See that?"

"Oh-ho," Vecherovsky said respectfully.

We admired the box.

"Greetings from the supercivilization," I said. "Oh, yes! What were you saying? He mixed me up completely. Oh, I remember! You mean, after all of this, you still maintain—"

"Mm-hmm. I still maintain. I always knew that there were no supercivilizations. And now, after all this, as you put it, I am beginning to guess why they don't exist."

"Hold on." I put down the cup. "Why, et cetera, et cetera—that's all theoretical. You tell me this: If it isn't a supercivilization, if it isn't aliens, then who is it?" I was angry. "Do you know something or are you just exercising your tongue, amusing yourself with paradoxes? One man shot himself, another's turned into a jellyfish. What are you blathering about?"

No, even to the naked eye it was obvious that Vecherovsky wasn't amusing himself with paradoxes or blathering. His face suddenly went gray and tired-looking, and then an enormous, carefully concealed tension surfaced. Or maybe it was stubbornness—savage, tenacious stubbornness. He stopped looking like himself. His face was usually rather wilted, with a sleepy aristocratic flabbiness—now it was rock hard. And I was frightened again. For the first time it occurred to me that Vecherovsky wasn't sitting with me to give me moral support. And that wasn't why he had invited me to spend the night, and earlier, to sit and work in his apartment. And even though I was very frightened, I suddenly felt a wave of pity for him,

based on nothing, really, just on some vague feelings and on
the change in his face.

And then I remembered, for no reason at all, that three
years ago Vecherovsky had been hospitalized, but not for
long . . .

Excerpt 17. . . . a previously unknown type of benign tumor.
And I found out about it only last fall, yet I saw him every
blessed day, had coffee with him, listened to his Martian guffaws, complained that I was tired of hearing about his problems. And I didn't suspect a single thing, not a thing.

And now, overwhelmed by that unexpected pity, I couldn't
stop myself, and I said, knowing that it was pointless, that I
would get no answer:

"Phil, are you, are you under pressure too?"

Of course, he paid no attention to my question. He simply
didn't hear it. The tension left his face and disappeared in the
aristocratic puffiness, his reddish lids settled back down over
his eyes, and he resumed puffing on his pipe.

"I'm not blathering at all," he said. "You're driving yourself
crazy. You invented your supercivilization, and you can't understand that it's too simple; that it's contemporary mythology
and nothing more."

My skin crawled. More complex? Worse, then? What
could be worse?

"You're an astronomer," he continued reproachfully. "You
should know about the fundamental paradox of xenology."

"I know it. Any civilization in its development is very
likely—"

"And so on," he interrupted. "It's inevitable that we would
observe traces of their activity, but we do not. Why? Because
there are no supercivilizations. Because for some reason civilizations do not become supercivilizations."

"Yes, yes. The idea that reason destroys itself in nuclear wars. That's a lot of nonsense."

"Of course it's nonsense," he agreed calmly. "It's also too simplified, too primitive—in the realm of our usual way of thinking."

"Wait. Why do you keep harping on primitive? Of course, nuclear war is a primitive concept. But it needn't be that simple. Genetic diseases, some boredom with existence, a reorientation of goals. There's a whole literature on this. I for one feel that manifestations of supercivilizations are cosmic in nature, and we just can't distinguish them from natural cosmic phenomena. Or take our situation, for instance, why do you say it isn't a manifestation of a supercivilization?"

"Hmm, too human. They've discovered that earthlings are on the threshold of the universe. Afraid of the competition, they decide to stop it. Is that it?"

"Why not?"

"Because that's fiction. Dime-store fiction in bright, cheap covers. It's like trying to fit an octopus into a pair of tuxedo pants. And not a plain octopus at that, but an octopus that doesn't even exist."

Vecherovsky moved the cup, put his elbow on the table, and, resting his chin on his fist and raising his eyebrows high, stared above my head into space.

"Look how it turns out. Two hours ago we seemed to have come to some decision. It doesn't matter what force is operating on us, the important thing is how to behave under that pressure. But I see that you're not thinking about that at all; you stubbornly keep trying to identify the force. And just as stubbornly, you return to the hypothesis about the supercivilization. You are prepared to forget—and have already forgotten—your own feeble objections to this hypothesis. I can understand why this is happening to you. Somewhere in the back of your mind you have the idea that any supercivilization is still a civilization, and two civilizations can always come to an accord, find some sort of compromise, feed the wolves and save the sheep. And if worse comes to worst, there is always sweet surrender to this hostile but imposing power, noble retreat before an enemy worthy of victory, and then— how the devil does play tricks—maybe even a reward for your reasonable docility. Don't bug your eyes out at me, Dmitri. I said this was all subconscious. And do you think you're the only one? It's a very, very human trait. We've rejected God, but we still can't stand on our own two feet without some myth-crutch to hold us up. But we'll have to. We'll have to learn. Because in your situation, not only do you not have any friends, you are so alone that *you don't have any enemies, either*! That's what you refuse to understand."

Vecherovsky stopped. I had tried to interrupt him, tried to find arguments to refute his point, to argue heatedly, foaming at the mouth—but to prove what? I don't know. He was right. It's no shame to concede to a worthy opponent. I mean, that's not what he thought, that's what I think, that is, what I suddenly just thought, after he said it. I've had this feeling all along that I'm the general of a decimated army wandering around in the fire, looking for the victorious general to hand over my sword. That I'm less bothered by my position than by the fact that I can't find the enemy.

"What do you mean there is no enemy?" I finally said. "Somebody wanted all of this."

"And who wanted it to be," Vecherovsky drawled, "for a rock near the Earth's surface to fall with an acceleration of nine point eight one?"

"I don't understand."

"But it does fall precisely at that rate?"

"Yes."

"And you don't drag a supercivilization into the case? To explain that fact."

"Wait. What does that have—"

"So who wanted the rock to fall with precisely that acceleration? Who?"

I poured myself some tea. It seemed as though all I had to do was add two and two, but I still didn't understand a thing.

"You mean that we're dealing with some sort of elemental force? A natural phenomenon?"

"If you like," Vecherovsky said.

"Well, really!" I spread out my hands, knocking over my tea and spilling it all over the table. "Damn!"

While I cleaned up the table, Vecherovsky continued lazily: "Try to recant epicycles, and try to put the Sun, rather than the Earth, at the center of things. You'll see how it falls into place."

I threw the wet rag into the sink.

"You mean you have a theory," I said.

"Yes, I do."

"Well, let's hear it. By the way, why didn't you tell us right away? While Weingarten was here?"

Vecherovsky's eyebrows wiggled.

"You see, every new theory has a drawback—it always creates a lot of arguments, and I didn't feel like arguing. I just wanted to assure you that you were faced with a choice and that each of you had to make that choice alone, on your own. Apparently, I didn't succeed. And I guess my theory could have served as an additional argument, because its gist—in fact, the only possible conclusion that can be made from it—is that you now not only have no friends, but you also have no enemy. So perhaps I was wrong. Perhaps I should have gotten into an exhausting discussion, that would have made your position clearer. Things as I see them are like this . . ."

I can't say that I didn't understand his theory, but I can't say that I fully grasped it either. I can't say that this theory convinced me fully, but on the other hand everything that had happened to us fit into it nicely. More than that, everything that ever happened, was happening, and will ever happen in the entire universe fit into it—that was the theory's weakness. It smacked of the statement that rope was simply rope.

Vecherovsky introduced the concept of the Homeostatic Universe. "The universe retains its structure," that was his fundamental axiom. In his words, the laws of conservation of energy and matter were simply discrete manifestations of the law of conservation of structure. The law of nondecreasing entropy contradicts the homeostasis of the universe and therefore is a partial law and not a universal one. Complementary to this law is the law of constant reproduction of reason. The combination and conflict of these two partial laws are an expression of the universal law of the conservation of structure.

If only the law of nondecreasing entropy existed, the structure of the universe would disappear and chaos would reign. But on the other hand, if only a constantly self-perfecting and all-powerful intelligence prevailed, the structure of the universe based on homeostasis would also be disrupted. This, of course, did not mean that the universe would become better or worse—merely different—contrary to the principle of homeostasis, since a constantly developing intelligence can have but one goal: to change nature. That is why the gist of the Homeostatic Universe consists in maintaining the balance between the increase in entropy and the development of reason. That is why there are no and can be no supercivilizations, since the term *supercivilization* is used for intelligence developed to such a degree that it transcends the law of nondecreasing entropy on a cosmic scale. And what was happening to us now was nothing other than the first reaction of the

Homeostatic Universe to the threat of humanity becoming a supercivilization. The universe was defending itself.

Don't ask me, Vecherovsky said, why you and Glukhov became the first swallows of the coming cataclysm. Don't ask me about the physical nature of the signals that disturbed the homeostasis in that corner of the universe where you and Glukhov undertook your research. In fact, don't ask me about any of the mechanisms of the Homeostatic Universe—I know nothing about them, the way people know nothing about the functioning of the law of the conservation of energy. All processes occur in such a way as to conserve energy. All processes occur in such a way that in a billion years from now the work by you and Glukhov, when combined with the work of millions upon millions of other people, does not lead to the end of the world. Of course, it is not a question of the end of the world in general but of the end of the world as we observe it today, the world as it has existed for a billion years, the world that you and Glukhov, without even suspecting it, are threatening with your microscopic attempts to overcome entropy.

That's sort of what I understood, though I'm not sure I got it completely right; I could be completely wrong. I didn't even argue with him. It was bad enough without this, but looking at it this way made everything so hopeless that I just didn't know how to react—why go on living? God! D. A. Malianov versus the Homeostatic Universe! This isn't even being a bug under a brick. It's not even a virus in the center of the Sun . . .

"Listen," I said. "If that's really the way it is, what is there to talk about? The hell with my M cavities. Choice! What kind of choice can there be?"

Vecherovsky slowly removed his glasses and rubbed the irritated bridge of his nose with his pinkie. He was silent for a very long, exhaustingly long time. And I waited. My sixth sense told me that Vecherovsky wouldn't just drop me like this, to be devoured by his homeostasis; he would never have told me if there wasn't some way out, some variant, some choice, goddamn it. And when he finished rubbing his nose, he put his glasses back on and spoke in a quiet voice:

" 'I was told that this road would take me to the ocean of death, and turned back halfway. Since then crooked, round-about, godforsaken paths stretch out before me.' "

"Well?" I asked.

"Shall I repeat it?" Vecherovsky asked.

"Well, repeat it."

He repeated it. I wanted to cry. I got up quickly, filled the teakettle, and put it on the range.

"It's a good thing tea exists. Otherwise I'd be roaring drunk under the table by now," I said.

"I prefer coffee."

And then I heard a key turning in the lock. I must have turned white, or maybe blue, because Vecherovsky moved to-ward me and said quietly:

"Easy, Dmitri, easy. I'm here."

I barely heard him.

In the foyer another door opened, clothes rustled, quick footsteps, Kaliam's wild meows, and while I was still dumb-struck, I heard Irina's breathless "Kaliamkins." And then:

"Dmitri!"

I don't remember how I got out into the foyer. I grabbed Irina, hugged her, held her (Irina, Irina!), inhaled her familiar perfume—her cheeks were wet; she was muttering something strange: "You're alive, thank God. And I thought ... Dmitri!" Then we came to our senses. Anyway, I did. I mean, I fully realized that she was there and what she was saying. And my amorphous wooden terror was quickly replaced by a concrete everyday fear. I set her down, stepped back, looked into her tear-stained face (she wasn't even wearing makeup):

"What's wrong, Irina? Why are you here? Is it Bobchik?"

I don't think she was listening to me. She was grabbing my hands, feverishly looking into my face with her wet eyes, and repeating:

"I was going crazy ... I thought I'd be too late ... What's going on?"

Holding hands, we squeezed into the kitchen. I seated her on my stool, and Vecherovsky poured her some strong tea straight from the pot. She drank it greedily, spilling half of it on her coat. She looked horrible. I barely recognized her. I started shaking, and I leaned on the sink.

"Something happen to Bobchik?" I asked, barely managing to make my tongue work.

"Bobchik?" she repeated. "What does Bobchik have to do with this? I almost went crazy worrying about you. What's been going on here? Were you sick?" She was shouting. "You're as healthy as a bull!"

I felt my jaw drop, and I shut my mouth. I didn't understand a thing. Vecherovsky asked very calmly:

"Did you get bad news about Dmitri?"

She stopped looking at me and turned to him. Then she leaped up, ran into the foyer, and came back, rummaging through her purse.

"Just look, look at what I received." A comb, lipstick, papers, and money spilled on the floor. "God, where is it? Here!" She threw the purse on the table, stuck her trembling hand into her pocket (she missed on the first try), and pulled out a crumpled telegram. "Here."

I grabbed it. Read it. Understood nothing: IN TIME SNE-GOVOI. I read it again, and then, in desperation, out loud:

" 'DMITRI BAD HURRY TO MAKE IT IN TIME SNEGO-VOI.' Why Snegovoi? How could it be Snegovoi?"

Vecherovsky carefully took the telegram from me.

"Sent this morning," he said.

"When?" I asked loudly, like a deaf man.

"This morning. At nine twenty-two."

"God! Why would he play a trick like that on me?" she ...

CHAPTER 9

Excerpt 18. ... then me. She couldn't reach me by phone. She couldn't get a ticket at the airport. She stormed the director's office, brandishing the telegram, and he gave her a note, but it wasn't much help. There were no planes ready for takeoff, and the ones that arrived were going the wrong way. Finally, in desperation, she took a plane to Kharkov. Then the whole story started over again, but it was pouring rain there to boot. It was only toward evening that she managed to get to Moscow by a freight plane that was carrying refrigerators and coffins. From Domodedovo Airport she rushed over to Sheremetyevo, and she finally got to Leningrad riding in the cockpit. She hadn't eaten a single thing since she left and spent most of the time weeping. Even as she was falling asleep, she kept threatening to go to the post office first thing in the morning with the police and find out whose work it was, what bastards were responsible. Naturally, I agreed with her, saying, of course, we won't leave it at this; for jokes like this people should be punched out; no, more than that, they should be arrested. Of course, I didn't tell her that nowadays, thank God, the post office wouldn't accept a telegram like that without confirmation, that it is impossible to play practical jokes like that, and that it was most likely that no one sent the telegram, that the Teletype in Odessa just printed it out by itself.

I couldn't fall asleep. It was morning anyway. It was light

outside, and despite the blinds the room was bright. I lay still in bed, petting Kaliam, stretched out between us, and listened to Irina's even breathing. She always slept deeply and with great pleasure. There was nothing so bad in the world that it would give her insomnia. At least, so far there hadn't been.

The sickening sense of impending doom that befell me the moment I read and finally understood the telegram had not left me. My muscles were in cramps and inside, in my chest and stomach, was a huge, shapeless cold lump. Once in a while the lump moved, and then my skin crawled.

At first, when Irina fell asleep in mid-word and I heard her even breathing, for a moment I felt better. I wasn't alone. Next to me was the person nearest and dearest to me. But the cold toad in my chest stirred and I was horrified by that sense of relief; so this is what I've sunk to; they've reduced me to this: I can be happy that Irina is here, that Irina is in the same foxhole under fire with me. Oh no, we go for her ticket first thing in the morning. Back to Odessa. I'll push everyone aside, I'll chew our path through the lines to the ticket office.

My poor little girl, how she suffered because of those bastards, because of me and that lousy interstellar matter, all of which isn't worth a single wrinkle on Irina's face. And they got to her, too. Why? They needed her for something? The bastards, the blind bastards. They hit anyone who is in firing range. No, nothing will happen to her. They're just using her to scare me. They're playing on my nerves, one way or another.

Suddenly, I pictured dead Snegovoi—walking along Moscow Boulevard in his striped pajamas, heavy, cold, with a clotted bullet hole in his thick skull; coming into the post office and getting in line at the telegram window; a gun in his right hand, the telegram in his left; and nobody notices. The girl takes the telegram from his dead fingers, writes out a receipt, and, forgetting the money, calls out: Next.

I shook my head to dispel the vision, quietly got out of bed, and padded to the kitchen in my underwear. It was sunny in there, the sparrows were making a racket in the yard, and I could hear the janitor's broom. I picked up Irina's purse, fished out a crumpled pack with two broken cigarettes in it, sat down, and lit up. I hadn't smoked in a long time. Two, maybe three years. Proving my willpower. Yep, brother Malianov, you'll need your willpower now. Hell, I'm a lousy actor, and I don't know how to lie. Irina must know nothing. She has nothing to do with it. I have to do this alone. No one can help me, not Irina, no one.

And what does help have to do with it, anyway? Who's talking about help? I don't tell Irina my problems if I can at all avoid it. I don't like making her sad. I love making her happy and hate making her sad. If it weren't for all this crap I would have loved to have told her about the M cavities, she would have understood immediately, even though she's no theoretician and is always putting down her own abilities. But what can I tell her now?

There are different problems, however, different levels of problems. There are minor ones that it's no sin to complain about, that are even pleasant to kvetch about. Irina would say: Big deal, what nonsense, and everything would get better. If the problems are bigger, then it's just unmanly to talk about them. I don't tell Mother or Irina about them. And then there are the problems of such magnitude that it becomes a little unclear. First of all, whether I want it or not, Irina is in the firing line with me.

Something very unfair is happening here. I'm being battered to death, but at least I understand for what, can guess who's doing it, and know that I'm being battered. These are not stupid jokes and not fate; they're aiming at me. I think it's better to know that they're aiming at you. Of course, it takes all kinds, and probably most people would rather not know, but my Irina is not one of them. She's reckless; I know her. When she's afraid of something she rushes headlong right into her fear. It would be dishonest not to tell her. And in general, I have to make a decision. (I haven't even tried to think about that yet, and I'll have to. Or have I already chosen? Have I made my choice without knowing it?) And if I have to choose—well, let's assume the choice itself is up to me alone. We'll do what we want. But what about the consequences? One choice will lead to their tossing atom bombs, instead of plain ones, at us. Another choice—I wonder, would Irina have liked Glukhov? I mean he's a nice, pleasant man, quiet, meek. We could get a television, to Bobchik's everlasting joy; we could ski every Saturday, go to the movies. One way or the other the decision will affect more than just me. Sitting under a shower of bombs is bad, but finding out after ten years of marriage that your husband is a jellyfish is no picnic either. But maybe it would be all right. How do I know what she sees in me? That's just it, I don't. And maybe she doesn't know either.

I finished the cigarette and flipped the butt into the garbage. A passport lay next to the can. Nice. We had cleaned up every last scrap, every penny, but there was her passport. I picked up the gray-green book and looked at the first page distractedly. I don't know why. I broke out in a cold sweat. Sergeenko, Inna Fedorovna. Date of birth: 1939. What's this? The photograph was of Irina—no, not Irina. Some woman who looked like Irina, but wasn't. Some Sergeenko, Inna Fedorovna.

I carefully put the passport on the edge of the table and tiptoed to the bedroom. I broke out in another sweat. The woman lying under the sheet had dry skin, pulled taut on her face, and her upper teeth, white and sharp, were exposed, either in a smile or in a martyred grin. That was a witch there under my sheets. Forgetting myself, I shook her by her naked shoulder. Irina woke up immediately, opened her huge eyes, and muttered: "Dmitri, what's the matter? Does something hurt?" God, it was Irina. Of course it was Irina. What a nightmare. "I was snoring, right?" she asked in a sleepy voice and went back to sleep.

I tiptoed back to the kitchen, moved the passport away from me, took out the last cigarette, and lit up. Yes. That's how we live now. That's what our life will be now. From now on.

The icy animal inside me stirred some more, and then was still. I wiped the disgusting sweat from my face; I had an idea and started digging through her purse. Irina's passport was in there. Malianova, Irina Ermolaevna. Date of birth: 1933. Damn! All right, why did they need to do that? This was no accident. The passport, the telegram, Irina's difficult journey, the fact that she had to fly in a plane with coffins—all that wasn't accidental. Or was it? They were blind, Mother Nature, brainless natural elements. That's a good case for Vecherovsky's theory. If it was the Homeostatic Universe quelling a microrebellion, that's just how it should have seemed. Like a man swatting a fly with a towel—vicious, whistling blows cutting through the air; vases tumbling from shelves; lamps breaking; innocent moths falling victim to the blows; the cat, its paw stomped on, making a beeline for the couch. Massed power and inefficiency. I mean, I really don't know anything. Maybe somewhere on the other side of town a house collapsed. They were aiming for me and hit the house instead. And all I got was the crummy passport. And all this because I thought of the M cavities the other day? To think that I could have told Irina about them!

Listen, I probably won't be able to live like this. I never thought of myself as a coward, but living like this, without a moment's peace, terrified by your own wife because you've taken her for a witch. And Vecherovsky despises Glukhov.

That means he'll stop seeing me, too. I'll have to change everything. Everything will be different. Different friends, different work, a different life. Maybe even a different family. "Since then crooked, roundabout, godforsaken paths stretch out before me." And you'll be ashamed to look at yourself in the mirror when you're shaving in the morning. The mirror will reflect a very small and very tame Malianov.

Of course, you can get used to it, you can probably get used to everything in the world. To any waste. But this would be no little waste. I've spent ten years working toward this. More than ten years—my whole life. Since childhood, since the school science club, since the homemade telescopes, since the calculations of Wolfe's numbers according to someone's observations. My M cavities, I really don't know anything about them: what I might have done with them; what someone else might have done with them after me; continuing, developing, adding to it and passing it on to another age, the next century. Probably something not so minor might have come of it; I was losing something not so minor if it could lead to revelations that the universe itself is trying to stop. A billion years is a long time. In a billion years a civilization develops from a blob of slime—

But they'll squash me. First they won't let me live in peace, they'll drive me crazy, and if that won't work, they'll simply squash me. Oh boy! Six o'clock. The sun was broiling already.

And then, I don't know why, the cold animal in my chest disappeared. I stood up. Moving calmly, I went into the room and got my papers and a pen from the desk. I went back to the kitchen, settled down, and started to work.

I couldn't think well—my head was stuffed with cotton and my eyelids burned—but I carefully went through my notes, throwing out everything that was no longer necessary, put the rest in order, and copied it all into a notebook, slowly, with pleasure, carefully choosing my words, as though I were writing a final draft of an article or a report.

A lot of people don't like this stage of the work, but I do. I like polishing my terms, savoring the choice of the most elegant and economic turns of phrase, catching the mistakes hidden in the notes, plotting graphs, preparing tables. This is the scientist's noble dirty work—the summation, a time for admiring oneself and one's handiwork.

And I admired myself and my handiwork until Irina was next to me—hugging me with her bare arm and pressing her warm cheek against mine.

"Huh?" I said and straightened my back.

It was my usual Irina, and not that pathetic scarecrow she resembled yesterday. She was rosy and fresh, clear-eyed and jolly. A lark. She's a lark. I'm an owl, and she's a lark. I'd read about a classification like that somewhere. Larks go to bed early, sleep readily and with great pleasure, and wake up fresh and happy and start singing right away, and there's nothing in the world that will make them sleep until noon.

"You didn't sleep at all again?" she asked, and without waiting for an answer went to the balcony door. "What are they hollering about?"

I only then realized that there was a ruckus in our courtyard—the kind of crowd noises heard at the scene of an accident after the police have arrived and before the ambulance.

"Dmitri!" Irina shouted. "Look! Talk about miracles!"

My heart fell. I know those miracles. I jumped up . . .

Excerpt 19. . . . some coffee. And Irina announced cheerfully that everything had worked out marvelously. Finally, everything in the world was turning out marvelously. She had gotten sick of Odessa over those ten days because this summer it was more crowded than ever. She missed me and had no intention of going back to Odessa, particularly since she'd never be able to get a ticket, and her mother was planning to come to Leningrad in August; she could bring Bobchik then. Now she was going back to work, right now, as soon as she'd had her coffee, and in March or April we'd go skiing together in Kirovsk as we had planned.

We had a tomato omelet. While I cooked it, Irina combed the whole apartment looking for cigarettes, didn't find any and got a little blue, made more coffee, and asked about Snegovoi. I told her what I knew from Zykov—carefully avoiding all sharp angles and trying to present it as the usual tragic story. I remembered the beautiful Lidochka in the middle of my tale and almost brought her up but bit my tongue.

Irina was saying something about Snegovoi, remembered something, and the corners of her mouth drooped sadly ("... now there's nobody to borrow a cigarette from!"), and I sipped my coffee, thinking about what to do next. Until I decided to tell Irina or not, it was probably better not to mention Lidochka or the grocery order since that whole matter was rather unclear, or should I say very clear, since in all this time Irina hadn't said a word about her friend or her grocery order. Of course, Irina might have forgotten. First of all, all that anxiety, and second of all, Irina always forgets everything, but for the time being—Satan, get thee behind me—it was better to skirt the issues. Well, maybe it was better to send out a small trial balloon.

Choosing an appropriate moment, when Irina had stopped talking about Snegovoi and had gone on to cheerier topics, how Bobchik had fallen into a ditch and my mother-in-law after him, I asked casually:

"Well, and how's Lidochka doing?"

My small trial balloon turned out to be on the huge and clumsy side. Irina's eyes bulged.

"Which Lidochka?"

"You know, your school friend."

"Ponomareva? What made you think of her?"

"Oh, you know," I mumbled. "Just thought of her." I hadn't anticipated that question. "You know, Odessa, the battleship *Potemkin*. Just remembered her, that's all. Why the third degree?"

Irina blinked a few times and then said: "I ran into her. She's so beautiful now, has to beat men off with a stick."

There was a pause. Damn it, I just can't lie. Some trial balloon. Got it right between the eyes. Under Irina's inquisitive gaze, I put my empty cup on the saucer and said in a phony voice, "I wonder how our tree is doing?" and went over to the balcony. Well, it was all clear about Lidochka now. Definitely. And how was our tree doing?

The tree was in place. The crowd was thinning. There was only the doorman, three janitors, the plumber, and two cops. There was also a yellow patrol car down there. All of them (except for the car, of course) were looking at the tree and exchanging opinions on what to do and what it meant. One of the cops had removed his cap and was wiping his shaved head with a handkerchief. It was getting hot in the yard, and the familiar odor of heated asphalt, dust, and gasoline had a new strain in it—woodsy and strange. The shaved cop put his cap back on, put away the handkerchief, and dug his finger in the fresh dirt. I stepped away from the balcony.

Irina was in the bathroom. I cleared and washed the dishes. I was terribly sleepy, but I knew I wouldn't fall asleep. I probably wouldn't sleep until this whole thing was over. I called Vecherovsky. As soon as I heard the ring, I remembered that he wasn't supposed to be home today, he was giving exams to graduate students, but before I could hang up he answered.

"You're home?" I asked stupidly.

"What can I say?" Vecherovsky replied.

"All right, all right. Did you see the tree?"

"Yes."

"What do you think?"

"I think so."

I glanced over toward the bathroom and, lowering my voice, said:

"I think it's me."

"Yes?"

"Uh-huh. I decided to bring my notes into order."

"Did you?"

"Not completely. I'm going to try to finish up today."

Vecherovsky was silent.

"What for?" he asked.

I was stumped.

"I don't know, I wanted to clean it all up, all of a sudden. I don't know. Regret, I guess. I felt sorry for my work. Aren't you going out today?"

"I don't think so. How's Irina?"

"Chattering and chirping," I said. I smiled involuntarily. "You know Irina. Like water off a duck's back."

"You told her?"

"Are you kidding? Of course not."

"Why 'of course'?"

I sighed.

"You see, Phil, I keep thinking about it myself. Should I tell her or not? I can't figure it out."

"When in doubt," Vecherovsky declared, "do nothing."

I was going to tell him that that was a piece of information I had learned without him when I heard Irina turn off the shower. I mumbled into the phone:

"Okay, I'm going to work now. If there's anything, call me, I'll be home."

Irina got dressed and made up, kissed me on the nose, and hopped off. I lay back on the bed, cradling my head, and started to think. Kaliam appeared immediately, climbed up on me, and spread out along my side. He was soft, hot, and damp, and I fell asleep. It was like passing out. My consciousness disappeared, and then suddenly reappeared. Kaliam was no longer on the bed, and someone was ringing the doorbell. With the signal ta ta-ta ta-ta. I stood up. My head was clear, and I felt particularly scrappy. I was prepared for mortal combat and death. I knew that a cycle was beginning, but there was no more fear—just reckless, angry determination.

It was only Weingarten. A completely impossible thing: He was sweatier, messier, sloppier, and more unkempt than yesterday.

"What's that tree?" he demanded right in the doorway. And another impossibility: He was whispering.

"You can speak up," I said. "Come on in."

He came in, stepping gingerly and looking around, shoved two shopping bags with manuscripts into the closet, and wiped his wet neck with his wet hand. I pulled Kaliam back in by the tail and shut the door.

"Well?" Weingarten said.

"As you see," I replied. "Let's go to my room."

"Is the tree your work?"

"Mine."

We sat down. I sat at the table, Weingarten in the chair next to it. His huge hairy stomach peeked out from under his net T-shirt and unbuttoned nylon windbreaker. He wheezed, puffed, dried himself off, and then contorted his body, getting at the pack of cigarettes in his back pocket. And he muttered a chain of curses, directed at nothing in particular.

"The battle goes on, then," he finally said, exhaling thick streams of smoke through his hairy nostrils. "Better to die

standing up, ta-ta, than on your knees ... and all that. Jerk!"
he shouted. "Have you been downstairs? You idiot! Did you at
least see how it's growing? It was an explosion! And what if it
happened under your ass? Boom, ka-boom, and ta-ta!"

"What are you screaming for?" I asked. "Do you want
some valerian drops?"

"Have any vodka?"

"No."

"Some wine, then?"

"Nothing. What did you bring over for me?"

"My Nobel Prize!" he shouted. "I brought over my Nobel,
that's what! But not for you, you idiot! You have enough problems of your own." He attacked his jacket, pulling off the top
button and cursing. "There aren't too many idiots nowadays,"
he announced. "In our times, buddy, the majority quite rightly
supposes that it's better to be rich and healthy than poor and
sick. We don't need much: a trainload of bread and a trainload
of caviar, and the caviar can be black and the bread white.
This isn't the nineteenth century, buddy," he said sincerely.
"The nineteenth century is dead and buried, and everything
that's left of it is smoke and nothing more, buddy. I didn't sleep
all night. Zakhar snores and so does that freak son of his. I
spent the whole night bidding farewell to the remnants of the
nineteenth century in my consciousness. The twentieth century, buddy, is all calculation and no emotion! Emotion, as
we all know, is lack of information and nothing more. Pride,
honor, future generations—all aristocratic babble. Athos,
Porthos, and Aramis. I can't do that. I don't know how, ta-
ta! A question of values? If you like. The most valuable thing
in the world is my identity, my family, and my friends. The
rest can go to hell. The rest is outside the parameters of my
responsibility. Fight? Of course. For myself. My family; my
friends. To the end, without mercy. But for humanity? For the

dignity of earthlings? For galactic prestige? The hell with it! I don't fight for words! I have more important things to worry about. You can do as you like. But I don't recommend being an idiot."

He jumped up and headed for the kitchen, a huge dirigible in the hallway. Water gushed from the sink.

"Our entire everyday life," he shouted from the kitchen, "is a continuous chain of deals! You have to be a total idiot to make an unprofitable deal! They knew that even in the nineteenth century!" He stopped, and I could hear him gulping. Then the water stopped running, and Weingarten came back into the room, wiping his mouth. "Vecherovsky won't give you any good advice. He's a robot, not a man. And a nineteenth-century robot at that. If they had known how to make robots in the nineteenth century they would have made them like Vecherovsky. Look, you can consider me a vile person. I don't argue. But I'm not going to let anyone wipe me out; no one. Not for anything. A living dog is better than a dead lion. And a living Weingarten is a hell of a lot better than a dead Weingarten. That's Weingarten's point of view, and that of his family and friends, I trust."

I didn't interrupt. I've known that big-faced lug for a quarter century, and not just any century, but the twentieth. He was shouting like that because he had pigeonholed everything in his own mind. There was no point in interrupting, because he wouldn't have heard me. Until Weingarten has pigeonholed everything, you can argue with him as an equal, like with an ordinary mortal, and can even change his mind. But Weingarten, with everything settled, becomes a tape recorder on playback. Then he shouts and becomes inordinately cynical— probably stems from an unhappy childhood.

So I listened to him in silence, waiting for the tape to end, and the only strange thing was the number of times he referred to living and dead Weingartens. He couldn't have been frightened—he wasn't me, after all. I'd seen all kinds of Weingartens: Weingarten in love, Weingarten the hunter, Weingarten the coarse oaf, and Weingarten wiped out. But this was a Weingarten I'd never seen: a frightened Weingarten. I waited for him to turn himself off for a few seconds to get another cigarette and asked just in case:

"Did they frighten you?"

He dropped the cigarettes and gave me the finger, a big, wet finger, across the table. He had been waiting for the question. The answer had also been prerecorded, not only in gestures, but orally as well:

"I like that—frightened me!" he said, waving his finger under my nose. "This isn't the nineteenth century, you know. They used to frighten people in the nineteenth century. But they don't bother with that nonsense in the twentieth. In the twentieth, they buy you off. They didn't scare me, they bought me, understand, buddy? It's a nice choice! Either they flatten you into a pancake or they give you a spanking-new institute over which two scientists have already back-bitten each other to death. I'll do ten Nobel-winning projects at the institute, understand? Of course, the merchandise isn't all bad, either. It's sort of like my birthright. The right of Weingarten to have freedom of scientific curiosity. Not bad merchandise at all, buddy, don't argue with me. But it's been on the shelves too long. It belongs to the nineteenth century! Nobody has that freedom in the twentieth century anyway! You can take your freedom and spend all your life as a lab assistant, washing out test tubes. The institute is no mess of pottage, either! I'll start ten ideas there, twenty ideas, and if they don't like one or two, well, we'll bargain again. There's strength in numbers, buddy. Let's not spit into the wind. When a heavy tank is headed straight for you and the only weapon you have is the head on your shoulders, you have to know enough to jump out of its way."

He talked a lot longer, shouting, smoking, coughing hoarsely, running over to look into the empty bar, running away from it in disappointment, and shouting some more. Then he quieted down, ran out of words, leaned back in the armchair, rested his head on the back of the chair, and made distorted faces at the ceiling.

"All right, then," I said. "But where are you taking your Nobel Prize? You should have taken it down to the boiler room; instead you lugged it up five flights to my place."

"I'm taking it to Vecherovsky."

I was amazed.

"What's he going to do with your Nobel work?"

"I don't know. Ask him."

"Wait," I said. "Did he call you?"

"No, I called him."

"And?"

"What and?" He sat up in the chair and started buttoning his jacket. "I called him this morning and told him I choose the bird in hand."

"And?"

"What and? And ... he said, well then, bring your materials to me."

We sat in silence.

"I don't understand why he wants your materials."

"Because he is Don Quixote!" Weingarten barked. "Because he's never been pecked at by a barbecued chicken! Because he's never bitten off more than he can chew."

I suddenly understood.

"Listen, Val," I said. "Don't. The hell with him, he's gone nuts! They'll hammer him into the ground up to his neck! Who needs it?"

"What, then?" Weingarten asked greedily. "What?"

"Burn it, your damn revertase! Let's burn it right now. In the bathtub."

"Pity," Weingarten said and looked away. "What a pity. The work . . . it's first class. Extra special. Deluxe."

I shut up. And he was out of the chair again, running back and forth across the room, out into the hall and back, and his tape was back on again too. It's shameful, yes. Honor suffers, yes. His pride is hurt. Especially when you can't tell anyone about it. But if you think about it, pride is sheer lunacy and nothing else. Just driving himself mad. Why, most people wouldn't even think twice in our situation. And they'd call us idiots! And they'd be right. Have we never had to compromise before? Of course, hundreds of times! And will hundreds more! And not with gods, but with lousy bureaucrats, with nits who are too disgusting to touch.

His running in front of me, sweating and justifying himself, was getting me mad, and I said that it was one thing to compromise and another to capitulate. Oh, that did it! I got him badly. But I wasn't sorry in the least. It wasn't really him I was jabbing in the solar plexus, it was myself. Anyway, we had a fight, and he left. He took his bags and went up to Vecherovsky's. At the door he said he'd be back later, but I told him that Irina was back, and he collapsed completely. He doesn't like it when people don't like him.

I sat down at the desk and got to work. That is, not work, but organization. At first I kept expecting a bomb to go off under the table or a blue face with a noose around its neck to appear in my window. But nothing like that happened and I got caught up in the work, and then the doorbell rang again.

I didn't go to answer it right away. First I went to the kitchen and got the meat hammer—an ominous thing: one side has spikes and the other side is an ax. If something went wrong, I'd let him have it between the eyes. I'm a peaceful man, I don't like fights or arguments, or Weingarten either, but I'd had enough. Enough.

I opened the door. It was Zakhar.

"Hi, Dmitri, please, forgive me," he said with an artificial casualness.

I looked down the hall against my will, but there was no one else. Zakhar was alone.

"Come in, come in. Happy to see you."

"You see, I decided to look in on you." Still in that same artificial tone that didn't go at all with his shy smile and highly intelligent appearance. "Weingarten disappeared somewhere, damn him. I've been calling him all day, he's out. And since I was coming over to see Philip, I thought I'd look in here and see, maybe he was here."

"Philip?"

"No, no ... Valentin ... Weingarten."

"He went to Philip's," I said.

"Oh, I see!" Zakhar said with great joy. "Long ago?"

"Over an hour."

His face froze for a second when he saw the hammer in my hand.

"Fixing dinner?" he asked, and added, without waiting for an answer: "Well, I won't get in your way. I'm off." He started for the door, then stopped. "Oh yes, I almost forgot ... I mean, I didn't forget, I just don't know. Which is Philip's apartment?"

I told him.

"Ah, thank you. You see, he called and I ... somehow forgot to ask ... during the conversation."

He backed up to the door and opened it.

"I understand," I said. "And where's your boy?"

"It's all over for me!" he shouted joyfully, stepped over the threshold, and ...

CHAPTER 10

Excerpt 20. . . . get me to do a major cleanup of this goat's den. I barely got out of it. We agreed that I would finish my work, and Irina, since she had absolutely nothing else to do and was stir-crazy—she was incapable of just soaking in the tub and reading the latest issue of *Foreign Literature*—well, Irina would sort the laundry and take care of Bobchik's room. And I promised to do our room, but not today, tomorrow. *Morgen, morgen, nur nicht heute.* But it would sparkle spotlessly.

I settled in at my desk, and for a while everything was quiet and peaceful. I worked, and worked with pleasure, but it was an unusual sort of pleasure. I'd never experienced anything like it. I felt a strange, serious satisfaction, I was proud of myself and respected myself. I thought that a soldier who remains at the machine gun to cover his retreating comrades must feel like that. He knows he will be here forever, that he will never see anything other than the muddy field, the running figures in the enemy uniform, and the low, grim sky. And he also knows that it's right, that it can be no other way, and is proud of it. And some watchman in my brain carefully and sensitively listened and watched while I worked, remembered that nothing had finished, that it was all continuing, and that right in the desk drawer lay the fearsome hammer with the ax blade on one side and the spikes on the other. And the watchman made me look up, because something happened in the room.

Actually, nothing particular had happened. Irina was standing in front of the desk, looking at me. And at the same time something had happened, something unexpected and wild, because Irina's eyes were square and her lips were puffy. Before I could say anything Irina tossed a pink rag right on my papers, and as I picked it up I saw it was a bra.

"What's this?" I asked, absolutely bewildered, looking at Irina and back at the bra.

"What does it look like?" Irina said in a strange voice, turned her back to me, and went to the kitchen.

Chilled by premonitions, I toyed with the pink lacy garment and couldn't understand. What the hell? What does a bra have to do with anything? And then I remembered Zakhar's women. I got scared for Irina. I threw down the bra and raced into the kitchen.

Irina was sitting on a stool, leaning on the table, her head in her hands. A cigarette burned between the fingers of her right hand.

"Don't touch me," she said calmly and cuttingly.

"Irina!" I said pathetically. "Are you all right?"

"You animal ..." she muttered, pulled her hands away from her hair, and took a drag of the cigarette. I saw that she was crying.

An ambulance? That wouldn't help, who needs an ambulance? Valerian drops? Bromides? God, look at her face. I grabbed a glass and filled it with tap water.

"Now I understand everything," Irina said, inhaling nervously and pushing the glass away with her elbow. "The telegram and everything. Here we are. Who is she?"

I sat down and took a drink of the water.

"Who?" I asked dully.

For a second I thought she was going to hit me.

"That's really something, you noble bastard," she said in

disgust. "You didn't want to contaminate the connubial bed. How noble. So you took her into your son's bed."

I finished the water and tried to put down the glass but my hand wouldn't obey me. A doctor! I kept thinking. My poor Irina, I must get a doctor!

"All right," Irina said. She wasn't looking at me anymore. She was staring out the window and smoking, inhaling every few seconds. "All right, there's nothing to talk about. You always did say that love was an agreement. It always sounded so good: love, honesty, friendship. But you could have been more careful not to leave bras behind . . . Maybe there's a pair of panties, too, if we look hard enough?"

It came to me in a blinding flash. I understood it all.

"Irina! God. You scared me so badly. You gave me such a scare."

Of course, that wasn't at all what she expected to hear, because she turned to me, with her pale, beautiful, tearstained face, and looked at me with such expectancy and hope that I almost began to cry myself. She wanted only one thing: for this to be cleared up, explained away as nonsense, a mistake, a crazy coincidence, as soon as possible.

That was the last straw. I couldn't take it anymore. I didn't want to keep it to myself anymore. I dumped the whole horror story and the madness of the last two days on her.

My story must have sounded like a joke at first. But I went on talking, paying attention to nothing, not giving her a chance to get in sarcastic comments. I just poured it out, without any particular order, not worrying about chronology. I saw her expression of suspicion and hope change to amazement, then anxiety, then fear, and, finally, pity.

We were in our room by then in front of the open window—she was in the chair and I was on the rug, leaning my cheek against her knee; there was a storm outside. A purple cloud poured itself out over the rooftops, pelting rain, frantic lightning bolts attacking the high-rise's roof and disappearing into the building. Large cold drops fell on the windowsill and into the room. The wind gusts made the yellow drapes billow, but we sat motionless. She caressed my hair quietly. I felt enormous relief. I had talked it out. Gotten rid of half the weight. And I was resting, pressing my face against her smooth tan knee. The constant thunder made it hard to talk, but I had nothing else to say.

Then she said:

"Dmitri. You mustn't think about me. You must make your decision as though I didn't exist. Because I will be with you always anyway. No matter what you decide."

I hugged her tight. I guess I knew she would say that and I guess the words really didn't help, but I was grateful anyway.

"Forgive me," she said after a pause, "but I still don't have it quite clear in my own mind. No, I believe you, of course I do— it's just that it's all so terrible. Maybe there's some other explanation, something more, well, simple, more understandable. I guess I'm saying it wrong. Vecherovsky is right of course, but not about it being the—what did he call it?—the Homeostatic Universe. He's right that that's not the point. Really, what's the difference? If it's the universe, you have to give in; if it's aliens, you have to fight? But don't listen to me. I'm just talking because I'm confused."

She shivered. I got up, squeezed into the armchair with her and put my arms around her. All I wanted to do was tell her in every possible way how terrified I was. How terrified I was for myself, how terrified I was for her, how terrified I was for both of us. But that would have been pointless, and probably cruel.

I felt that if she didn't exist I would have known exactly what to do. But she existed. And I knew that she was proud of me, always had been. I'm a rather dull person and not too successful, but even I could be an object of pride. I was a good athlete, always knew how to work, had a good mind; I was in good standing at the observatory, in good standing among our friends; I know how to have a good time, how to be witty, how to handle myself in friendly arguments. And she was proud of all of that. Maybe just a little, but proud nevertheless. I could see her looking at me sometimes. I just don't know how she would react to my becoming a jellyfish. I probably wouldn't even be able to love her the right way anymore, I'd be incapable of that, too.

As though reading my mind, she said:

"Remember how happy we were that all our exams were behind us and that we'd never have to take one again to our dying day? It seems they're not all over. It seems there's still one more."

"Yes," I said and thought: But this is one test where nobody knows whether an A or a D is a better grade. And there's no way of knowing what gets you the A and the D.

"Dmitri," she whispered, her face close to mine. "You must really have invented something great for them to be after you. You really should be very proud, you and the others. Mother Nature herself is after you!"

"Hmmm," I said and thought: Weingarten and Gubar have nothing to be proud of anymore, and as for me, that's still moot.

And then, reading my mind once more, she said:

"And it's really not important what you decide. The important thing is that you're capable of such discoveries. Will you at least tell me what it's about? Or is that forbidden too?"

"I don't know," I said and thought: Is she just trying to console me or does she really feel that way; is she so terrified that she's trying to talk me into capitulating; is she merely trying to sweeten the pill that she knows I'll have to swallow? Or is she trying to get me to fight, is she getting my dander up?

"The pigs," she said softly. "But they won't break us up. Right? That, they'll never do. Right, Dmitri?"

"Of course," I said and thought: That's the whole issue, darling. That's what it's all about.

The storm was abating. The cloud was floating north, exposing a gray, misty sky from which fell a soft, gray rain.

"I brought the rain," Irina said. "And I was hoping that we could go to Solnechnoe on Saturday."

"It's a long way to Saturday," I said. "But maybe we should go."

Everything had been said. Now we had to talk about Solnechnoe, bookshelves for Bobchik, and the washing machine, which had conked out again. And we did talk about all that. And there was an illusion of a normal evening, and in order to extend and strengthen that illusion, we decided to have some tea. We opened a fresh pack of Ceylon, rinsed out the teapot with hot water in the most exacting and scientific manner, triumphantly placed the box of Pique Dame candies on the table, and watched the kettle, waiting for the moment of rolling boil. We made the same old jokes and set the table, and I quietly took the order blank from the deli and the note about Lidochka and I. F. Sergeenko's passport, crumpled them up, and stuffed them into the wastebasket.

And we had a marvelous teatime—it was real tea, an elixir—and talked about everything under the sun, except the most important thing. I kept wondering what Irina was thinking about, because she seemed to have been able to forget the whole nightmare—she told me everything that she thought about it and now had forgotten it with relief, leaving me alone, once again one on one with my decision.

Then she said she had to do the ironing and that I should sit with her and tell her something funny. I started clearing the table and the doorbell rang.

Humming a little tune, I headed for the foyer, giving Irina one quick look (she was very calmly wiping the chairs with a dry rag). Unlocking the door, I remembered my hammer, but it seemed melodramatic to go back for it, and I opened the door.

A very young tall man in a wet raincoat and with wet blond hair handed me a telegram and asked me to sign for it. I took his pencil stub, leaned the receipt against the wall, wrote the date and time at his prompting, signed it, returned the pencil and receipt, thanked him, and closed the door. I knew that it was nothing good. Right there in the foyer, under the harsh 200-watt bulb, I opened the telegram and read it.

It was from my mother-in-law. "BOBCHIK AND I LEAV-ING TOMORROW MEET FLIGHT 425 BOBCHIK SILENT VIOLATING HOMEOPATHIC UNIVERSE LOVE MAMA." And a strip of paper was glued on below: "HOMEOPATHIC UNI-VERSE STET." I read and reread the telegram, folded it in four, turned out the light, and went down the hall. Irina was wait-ing for me, leaning against the bathroom door. I handed her the telegram, said "Mama and Bobchik arrive tomorrow," and went straight to my desk. Lidochka's bra was draped across my notes. I put it neatly on the windowsill, gathered my notes, put them in order, and stuck them in my notebook. Then I got a fresh manila envelope, put everything inside, tied it, and, still standing, wrote on the face: "D. Malianov. On the Interac-tion of Stars and Interstellar Matter in the Galaxy." I reread it, thought a bit, and blacked out the "D. Malianov." Then I put the envelope under my arm and left. Irina was still by the bathroom door; the telegram was pressed to her chest. As I walked past, she made a feeble gesture with her hand, either to stop me or to thank me. I said, without looking at her: "I'm going to Vecherovsky's. I'll be back soon."

I went up the stairs slowly, step by step, hitching up the envelope, which kept slipping out from under my arm. For some reason the lights were out on the stairs. It was dim and very quiet, and I could hear through the open windows the water dripping from the roof. On the sixth-floor landing, by the garbage chute, where the lovers had been kissing, I stopped and looked out into the courtyard. The huge tree's damp leaves glistened black in the night. The yard was empty; the puddles shimmered, rippling in the rain.

I met no one coming down the stairs. But between the seventh and eighth floors a pathetic little man sat hunched up on the steps, with an old-fashioned gray hat next to him. I walked around him carefully and continued on, when he spoke:

"Don't go up there, Dmitri."

I stopped and looked at him. It was Glukhov.

"Don't go up there now," he repeated. "Don't!"

He got up, picked up his hat, straightened slowly, holding his back, and I saw that his face was smeared with something black—dirt or soot—his glasses were askew, and his lips were compressed tightly, as though he were in real pain. He fixed his glasses and spoke, barely moving his lips:

"Another envelope. White. Another flag of surrender."

I said nothing. He hit his hat against his knee, shaking off the dust, and then tried to clean it with his sleeve. He was silent too, but he didn't leave. I waited to see what he would say.

"You see," he said finally, "it's always unpleasant to capitulate. In the last century, they say, people shot themselves rather than capitulate. Not because they were afraid of torture or concentration camps, and not because they were afraid they'd crack under torture, but because they were ashamed."

"That happens in our century, too," I said. "And not so rarely."

"Yes, of course," he agreed. "Of course. It's very unpleasant for a person to realize that he's not at all what he thought he was. He wants to remain the way he was all his life, and that's impossible if he capitulates. And so he has to . . . And yet there's still a difference. In our century people shoot themselves because they're ashamed before others—society, friends . . . In the last century people shot themselves because they were ashamed before themselves. You see, for some reason, in our century, everybody thinks that a person can always come to terms with himself. It's probably true. I don't know why. I don't know what's going on here. Maybe it's because the world has become more complicated? Maybe it's because now there are so many other concepts besides pride and honor that can be used to convince people."

He looked at me expectantly, and I shrugged.

"I don't know. Maybe."

"I don't know, either. You would think I was an experienced capitulator, I've been thinking about it for so long, about nothing else, and I've come up with so many convincing arguments. You think that you've come to terms with it, you've calmed down, and then it starts up again. Of course there's a difference between the nineteenth and twentieth centuries. But a wound is a wound. It heals, disappears, and you forget all about it, then the weather changes, and it hurts. That's the way it's always been, in all centuries."

"I understand," I said. "I understand it all. But a wound is a wound. And sometimes another person's wound is much more painful."

"Dear God!" he whispered. "I'm not trying to . . . I would never dare. I'm just talking. Please don't think that I'm trying to talk you out of it, that I'm giving you any advice. Who am

I? You know, I keep thinking, what are we? I mean people like us? We're either very well brought up by our times and our country or else we're throwbacks, troglodytes. Why do we suffer so much? I can't figure it out."

I said nothing. He pulled on his funny hat with a weak, flabby gesture, and said:

"Well, good-bye, Dmitri. I guess we'll never see each other again, but it doesn't matter, it was very nice meeting you. And you do make excellent tea."

He nodded and started down the stairs.

"You could take the elevator," I told his receding back.

He didn't turn back and he didn't answer. I stood and listened to his footsteps, descending lower and lower, listened until I heard the door squeak open far below. Then it slammed shut, and everything was still again.

I readjusted the envelope under my arm, passed the last landing, and, holding on to the banister, completed the last flight of stairs. I stood and listened at Vecherovsky's door. Someone was in there. I could hear voices. Unfamiliar ones. I probably should come back another time, but I didn't have the strength. I had to finish it. And finish fast.

I rang the bell. The voices went on. I waited and then rang again, and didn't let go of the buzzer until I heard footsteps and Vecherovsky asking:

"Who's there?"

For some reason I wasn't surprised, even though Vecherovsky had always opened the door to everyone without ever asking anything. Like me. Like all my friends.

"It's me. Open up."

"Wait." There was silence.

There were no more voices, only the sound of someone many flights below opening the garbage chute. I remembered Glukhov's warning about going there now. "Don't go there,

Warmold. They want to poison you." What was that from? Something terribly familiar. The hell with it. I had nowhere else to go. And no time. I heard footsteps behind the door again and the lock turning. The door opened.

I reeled back involuntarily. I'd never seen Vecherovsky like that.

"Come in," he said hoarsely, and stepped aside to make way.

CHAPTER 11

Excerpt 21. . . . So you brought it anyway," Vecherovsky said.

"Bobchik," I said and put my envelope on the table.

He nodded and smeared the soot on his face with his dirty hand.

"I was expecting it," he said. "But not so soon."

"Who's here?"

"No one," he replied. "Just the two of us. Us and the universe." He looked at his dirty hands and made a face. "Excuse me, I'll wash up first."

He left, and I sat on the arm of the chair and looked around. The room looked as if a cartridge of black gunpowder had exploded in it. Black soot spots on the walls. Thin strings of soot floating in the air. An unpleasant yellow tinge on the ceiling. And an unpleasant chemical smell—sour and acrid. The parquet floor was ruined by a round, charcoal-dirty depression. And there was another one on the windowsill, as though they had lit a campfire on it. Yes, they really had given it to Vecherovsky.

I looked at the desk. It was heaped with papers. One of Weingarten's folders lay open in the center, and the other, still tied up, was next to it. And there was another one, an old-fashioned one with a marbleized cover and a label on which was typed: "USA-Japan. Cultural Interrelations. Materials." And there were pages covered with what I took to be electronic schematic drawings, and one was signed in a scratchy, fuddy-duddy handwriting, "Gubar, Z. Z.," and below it in block letters: "Fading." My new white envelope was on the edge of the desk. I picked it up and put it on my lap.

The water in the bathroom stopped running, and a little later Vecherovsky called me.

"Dmitri, come in here. We'll have some coffee."

But when I came into the kitchen, there was no coffee; instead, there was a bottle of cognac and two exquisite crystal glasses. Vecherovsky had not only washed up, but he had changed his clothes. He had replaced his elegant jacket with the huge hole under the breast pocket and his cream pants with a soft suede lounging outfit. And no tie. His washed face was unusually pale, which made his freckles stand out even more, and a lock of wet red hair fell over his knobby forehead. There was something other than the paleness that was unusual about his face. And then I realized that his brows and lashes had been singed. Yes, they had really given it to Vecherovsky.

"A tranquilizer," he said, pouring the cognac. "*Probst!*"

It was Akhtamar, a rare and legendary Armenian cognac. I took a sip and savored it. Marvelous cognac. I took another sip.

"You're not asking any questions," Vecherovsky said, looking at me through his glass. "That must be hard. Or is it?"

"No, I have no questions. For anybody." I leaned an elbow on my white envelope. "I do have an answer. And it's the only one. Listen, they're going to kill you."

He raised his singed eyebrows out of habit and took a sip from his glass.

"I don't think so. They'll miss."

"Sooner or later they won't miss."

"*A la guerre comme à la guerre,*" he countered and stood up. "All right, now that my nerves are soothed, we can have some coffee and discuss the whole thing."

I watched his rounded back and his mobile shoulder blades as he ministered to his coffee apparatus.

"There's nothing for me to discuss. I have Bobchik."

And my own words suddenly made something click for me. From the moment I read the telegram, all my thoughts and feelings had been anesthetized; now they suddenly defrosted and started working at full blast. The fear, loathing, despair, and feeling of impotence came back, and I realized with unbearable clarity that from that moment a line of fire and brimstone that could never be crossed was drawn between Vecherovsky and me. I would have to stop behind it for the rest of my life, while he went on through the land mines, dust, and mud of battles I would never know and disappeared in the flaming horizon. He and I would nod hello when we ran into each other on the stairs, but I would stay on this side of the line with Weingarten, Zakhar, and Glukhov—drinking tea or beer, or chasing vodka with beer, and gabbing about intrigues and promotions, saving up for a car, and eking out my existence over some dull, official project. And I would never see Weingarten and Zakhar either. We'd have nothing to say to each other; we'd be too embarrassed to meet, nauseated by the sight of each other, and we'd have to buy vodka or port wine to forget the embarrassment and nausea. Of course I'd still have Irina, and Bobchik would be alive and well, but he would never grow up to be the man I had wanted him to be. Because I would no longer have the right to want him to be that way. Because he would never be able to be proud of me. Because I would be that papa "who could have made a major discovery, too, but for your sake . . ." Damn that moment to hell when those stupid M cavities floated up in my brain!

Vecherovsky set the cup of coffee before me, sat down opposite me, and with a precise, elegant motion poured the rest of his cognac into his coffee.

"I'm planning to leave here," he said. "I'll probably leave the institute, too. I'll hole up somewhere far away. In the Pamirs, maybe. I know they need meteorologists for the fall-winter period."

"What do you know about meteorology?" I asked dully, while I thought: You won't get away from *it* in any Pamirs; they'll find you in the Pamirs, too.

"It's not a difficult profession," Vecherovsky countered. "There's no special qualification for it."

"It's stupid," I said.

"What is, precisely?"

"It's a stupid idea," I said. I did not look at him. "What good will it do if you become a routine technician instead of re-maining a mathematician? Do you think they won't find you? They will, and how!"

"And what do you suggest?"

"Throw it all in the incinerator," I said, barely able to talk. "Weingarten's revertase, and the Cultural Exchange, and this." I pushed the envelope toward him across the smooth tabletop. "Throw it all away and concentrate on your own work."

Vecherovsky looked at me in silence through his power-ful lenses, blinking with his singed lashes, then knitted the remains of his brows and stared into his cup.

"You are a top-notch specialist," I said. "You're the best in Europe!"

Vecherovsky was silent.

"You have your work!" I shouted, feeling my throat con-strict. "Work! Work, goddamn you! Why did you have to get mixed up with us?"

Vecherovsky gave a long, deep sigh, turned sideways to me, and leaned his head and back on the wall.

"So, you misunderstood," he said slowly, and there was an unusual and totally out-of-place smugness and satisfaction in his voice. "My work . . ." Without moving, he squinted an eye in my direction. "They've been after me for two weeks because of my work. You have nothing to do with it, my little lambs. You must admit that I have remarkable self-control."

"Drop dead," I said, and stood up to leave.

"Sit down!" I sat.

"Pour the cognac in the coffee!" I poured.

"Drink." I drained the cup, tasting nothing.

"You actor," I said. "There's a lot of Weingarten in you sometimes."

"Yes, there is. And of you, and Zakhar, and Glukhov. There's more of Glukhov in me than of anyone else." He carefully poured some more coffee. "Glukhov. The desire for a quiet life, for irresponsibility. Let's become the grass and the bushes, let's become water and flowers. I'm probably irritating you?"

"Yes."

He nodded: "That's only natural. But there's nothing you can do. I want to explain to you what's going on. You seem to think that I'm going to face a tank empty-handed. Nothing of the sort. We are dealing with the laws of nature. It's stupid to fight the laws of nature. It's shameful to capitulate before them and, in the long run, stupid, too. The laws of nature must be studied and then put to use. That's the only possible approach. And that's what I plan to do."

"I don't understand."

"You will in a minute. This law did not manifest itself before our time. To put it more accurately, we had never heard of it. Though it may be no accident that Newton got caught up in interpreting the Apocalypse and Archimedes was cut down by a drunken soldier. Anyway, those are random thoughts. The problem is that the law manifests itself in only one way— through unbearable pressure. Pressure that threatens your mind and even your life. But nothing can be done here. After all, that's not unique in the history of science. There was the same danger in researching radioactivity, defusing storms, in the theory that there are many inhabited worlds. Perhaps with time we will learn to channel this pressure into harmless areas, and maybe even to harness it for our own goals. But there's nothing you can do now, the risk must be taken—I repeat, not for the first and not for the last time in the history of science. I want you to understand that there is basically nothing new or unusual in this situation."

"Why do I have to understand that?" I asked grimly.

"I don't know. Maybe it'll make it easier for you. And then I would like you to know that this isn't for a day or for a year. I think that it may be for more than a century. There's no hurry," he snorted. "There's a billion years to go. But we can and must start now. And you ... well, you'll have to wait. Until Bobchik grows up. Until you get used to the idea. Ten years, twenty—it doesn't matter."

"It does, and how!" I said, feeling a disgusting crooked smirk on my face. "In ten years I won't be good for anything. And in twenty I won't give a damn about anything."

He didn't say anything; he shrugged and filled his pipe. We sat in silence. He was trying to help me. Paint some prospects for me, prove that I wasn't such a coward and that he wasn't such a hero. That we were just two scientists; we were offered a project, and due to circumstances, he could work on it now and I couldn't. But it didn't make it any easier for me. Because he was going to the Pamirs to struggle with Weingarten's re-vertase, Zakhar's fadings, with his own brilliant math, and all the rest. They would be aiming balls of fire at him, send-ing ghosts, frozen mountain climbers, especially female ones, dropping avalanches on him, tossing him in space and time, and they would finally get to him there. Or maybe not. Maybe

he would determine the laws of the manifestations of fire
and the invasions of frozen mountain climbers. And maybe
none of this would happen. Maybe he'd just sit and pore over
the work and try to discover the point of intersection of the
theory of M cavities and the qualitative analysis of Ameri-
can cultural influence on Japan, and probably that will be a
very strange point of intersection, and it's also probable that
he will find the key to the whole vicious mechanism in that
point, and maybe even the key to controlling the mechanism.
And I will stay home, meet my mother-in-law and Bobchik
at the plane tomorrow, and we'll all go out and buy the bookshelves together.

"They'll kill you there," I said hopelessly.

"Not necessarily," he said. "And after all, I won't be there
alone ... and not only there ... and not only me."

We looked into each other's eyes. Behind the thick lenses
there was no tension, no false fearlessness, no flaming martyr-
dom—only the reddish calmness and reddish confidence that
everything should be just the way it was and no other way.

And he said nothing else, but I felt that he was still speaking. There's no hurry, he was saying. There's still a billion years
to the end of the world, he was saying. There's a lot, an aw-
ful lot, that can be done in a billion years if we don't give up
and we understand, understand and don't give up. And I also
thought that he said: "He knew how to scribble on paper under the candle's crackle! He had something to die for by the
Black River." And his satisfied guffaws, like Wells's Martian
laughter, rang in my ears.

I lowered my eyes. I sat hunched up, clutching the white
envelope to my stomach with both hands and repeated for the
tenth time, the twentieth time: "Since then crooked, round-
about, godforsaken paths stretch out before me ..."

A NOTE FROM THE TRANSLATOR

Arkady and Boris Strugatsky are Russia's best-known science fiction writers. Intellectually invigorating, full of adventure, and set in fantasy worlds, their work was in fact powerful social criticism that could not be expressed more directly in other forms under Soviet censorship. Even so, they had to deal with censors for every publication. The brothers lived in different cities, Arkady in Moscow, Boris in Leningrad, and in those pre-Internet days, they met in person to work on their books, see publishers, and try to persuade editors to leave in concepts, phrases, even individual "suspect" words.

The collapse of the USSR brought an end to state censorship, and many new editions of the Strugatskys' previously expurgated works appeared. The canonic texts, edited and annotated by Boris Strugatsky, were published in 2000–2001. This edition of *Definitely Maybe* is based on those publications, and it is the first time the complete text has been available in English.

In this afterword, Strugatsky tells the backstory to *Definitely Maybe* (which was called *A Billion Years Before the End of the World* in Russian), and discusses the writing process from proposal to text, the delay caused by a political-literary case in which Boris was a witness, and the book's eventual publication. Boris refers to Arkady as AN and himself as BN; the "N" stands for Natanovich, their patronymic.

The case that delayed the writing of the book was that of Mikhail Kheifets, who was arrested for "spreading anti-Soviet propaganda" in 1974. Kheifets was charged with writing the introduction to a collection of poems by Joseph Brodsky and editing a collection of essays by Andrei Amalrik, both of which were samizdat editions. *Samizdat*, which literally means "self-published," was the method by which banned works were circulated in the Soviet Union: people typed manuscripts with as many carbon copies as possible and passed them around, and the recipients retyped more copies. Boris was called as a witness, and denied ever having seen the books. Kheifets was given four years in the camps.

After the death of his brother in 1991, Boris wrote under the pen name S. Vititsky, and *Search for Predestination, or the Twenty-Seventh Theorem of Ethics* (1995) deals with the KGB and the Kheifets case. Boris died in 2012.

Antonina W. Bouis

AN AFTERWORD TO *DEFINITELY MAYBE*

On April 23, 1973, this notation appeared in our work diary:

> Ark[ady] arrived to write a proposal for Aurora [publishing house].
> 1. "Faust, 20th century." Hell and Heaven try to stop the development of science.
> 2. A Billion Years Before the End of the World ("before the Final Judgment").
> Saboteurs
> The Devil
> Aliens
> Spiridon Octopi
> Union of the Nine
> The Universe

This was followed by a proposal that gave the essence and plot of the future novella in much detail and with great similarity to the final version. The rare case where we managed to build the "skeleton" of a novella in a single workday.

The further elaboration of the book was continued during a May meeting—we even began writing a rough draft and a dozen pages—but then we had to interrupt the work: first to work on the screenplay for *Fighting Cats* and then on the novella *The Kid from Hell*. It was only in June 1974, having rewritten the ten pages, that we took up *Billion* seriously and completed it in December.

Today I am certain that the delay of almost a year was only

beneficial. In the spring of 1974, BN was dragged into the so-called Kheifets affair: this was his first face-to-face confrontation with our valiant "competent organs"; fortunately, he was only called as a witness. This confrontation (described in a fair amount of detail by S. Vititsky in *Search for Predestination*) left an ineradicable mark on BN and colored (at least for him) the entire atmosphere of *Billion* in a completely specific way and with a completely specific tone. *Billion* became for BN (and naturally, according to the law of communicating vessels, for AN as well) a novella about the tormenting and essentially hopeless struggle of mankind to preserve the "right of primogeniture" against the dull, blind, persistent force that knows neither honor, nor nobility, nor charity, that knows only one thing—how to achieve its goals, by any means, without any setbacks. When we wrote this novella, we could clearly see the real and cruel proto-image of the Homeostatic Universe that we had invented, and we saw ourselves in the subtext, and we tried to be realistic and ruthless—toward ourselves and the entire invented situation from which there was only one exit, as in the real world—through the loss, total or partial, of self-respect. "If you have the guts to be yourself," as John Updike wrote, "other people'll pay your price."

Amazingly, even though the subtext of the novella seemed carefully hidden, it kept poking through uncontrollably and making the authorities wary. Thus, Aurora, which was waiting impatiently for our novella, and which had in fact commissioned it and even given us an advance, despite the good reviews, despite the absolute impossibility of picking on any specific thing as unacceptable, despite their original goodwill toward the authors—despite all this, they immediately demanded that the action be moved to some capitalist country ("the USA, for example"), and when the authors refused, they immediately rejected the novella, with regret but decisively.

We managed to get it published in the magazine *Znanie-sila*, and at the cost of relatively small changes. The first victim of the censors was naturally Lidochka's bra, which was declared a toxic bomb placed by the authors under the people's morality. . . . But most of all, I remember, we were surprised by the determined and totally uncompromising insistence that the warning telegram ("BOBCHIK SILENT VIOLATING HOMEOPATHIC UNIVERSE") be removed. It remains an editorial secret as to which higher-up had what "uncontrolled associations" with that telegram. They had at first demanded that we cut the Homeostatic Universe *en grand*, but we and our editor friends managed to fight them off with a relatively minor concession: getting rid of the concept of "homeostasis" (which for some reason the authorities imbued with a socio-mystical significance) and introducing the concept of "Preservation of the Structure" (apparently, this was devoid of all social-mystical spirit). We also had to change "criminal investigator" to "procuratorial investigator." Or the other way around. I don't remember. One of these investigators did not suit the overseers—which one? Why? God only knows. Or perhaps the devil; it's more in his line, I think.

I just had a thought: *all* the characters have a prototype. A rare case! No one is totally made up, except for Investigator Zykov, and even he is an average of Porfiry Petrovich (see *Crime and Punishment*) and the KGB investigator who was in charge of the Kheifets case. Perhaps that's why we always considered *Billion* one of our favorite novellas—it was a piece of our life, a very concrete, very personal life, filled with absolutely concrete people and real events. And as we all know, there is nothing more pleasurable than recalling unpleasantness that has bypassed us successfully.

Boris Strugatsky

THE NEVERSINK LIBRARY

THE NEVERSINK LIBRARY

THE NEVERSINK LIBRARY